"Roger Welsch is a funny
about making sure the tradi
are not soon forgotten. . .
in the good company of American regionalists whose catalog of life works span the nuts and bolts of a life well told. . . . Whether your copy sits by your bedside or toilet, on your coffee table or tractor seat, buy it, read it, and by all means share it."

—ELAINE EFF, Maryland folklorist

"Roger Welsch has his finger firmly on the pulse of rural Plains humor, because it's his own pulse. He knows this tradition from a life spent where it happens—in the field, the tavern, the church hall, and the pickup cab—and his ear is perfectly attuned to catch its modest, ribald hilarity."

—TIM LLOYD, executive director of the American Folklore Society

"I don't know which I admire more, Roger Welsch's life style or his prose style."

—CHRIS PORTERFIELD, writer for *Time* magazine, author, and producer

"It would be difficult to find a folklorist more prolific and more popular than Roger Welsch, or 'Captain Nebraska' as some have dubbed him with great affection, following his hugely successful years as a correspondent on CBS's Charles Kuralt show. . . . Readers in Nebraska and beyond will be pleased to see yet another volume of good-humored Plains folklore in this latest work collected by Roger Welsch."

—ELAINE J. LAWLESS, Curators' Distinguished Professor Emerita at the University of Missouri and past president of the American Folklore Society

"Roger Welsch is ready to deliver a smile when the moment is right. He is the Cialis of humor."

—MIKE PLEWS, member, RW Fan Club

"Welsch's book is 100 percent humor born of friendships in the taverns and communities of rural Nebraska. This folklore historian who has rugged good looks and a titanic sense of humor (and who owes me a drink) has knocked it out of the park—again."

—T. MARNI VOS, humorist and president of Laughter's Echo Inc.

"Three folklorists walk into a bar. One is Roger Welsch. The other two record every syllable of conversation, then analyze the texts and context, using all the esoteric scholarly terms possible. Roger, instead, quotes the stories, tells a few of his own, and explains clearly what is going on. Whose book would you rather read?"

—JAN BRUNVAND, American folklore scholar and author of *The Vanishing Hitchhiker* and other books on urban legends

BISON
BOOKS

Why I'm an Only Child and Other Slightly Naughty Plains Folktales

ROGER WELSCH

FOREWORD BY DICK CAVETT

University of Nebraska Press
Lincoln & London

Manufactured in the United States of America

Library of Congress Cataloging-in-Publication Data
Names: Welsch, Roger L., author. | Cavett, Dick, writer of added text.
Title: Why I'm an only child and other slightly naughty Plains folktales / Roger Welsch; foreword by Dick Cavett.
Description: Lincoln: University of Nebraska Press, 2016.
Identifiers: LCCN 2015024784
ISBN 9780803284289 (pbk.: alk. paper)
ISBN 9780803285910 (epub)
ISBN 9780803285927 (mobi)
ISBN 9780803285934 (pdf)
Subjects: LCSH: Welsch, Roger L. | Authors, American—20th century—Biography | Folklore—Nebraska. | Nebraska—Social life and customs.
Classification: LCC PS3573.E4944 W58 2016 | DDC 398.20978—dc23 LC record available at http://lccn.loc.gov/2015024784

Set in ITC New Baskerville by L. Auten.

For Linda, the wit and soul of my life

Contents

Foreword

DICK CAVETT

The prolific sage of Dannebrog, Nebraska, has done it again.

What we have here is a work for the ages. It should be called a rescue operation. A heroic rescue of a rich trove of hilarious material from a largely unheralded and neglected and wholly American phenomenon called Plains humor.

For recognizing its unique value and lovingly collecting it, we owe the author, as you will happily discover, a deep thanks. With this book, you will be a pleased benefactor of Roger Welsch's painstaking and scholarly work. In simpler terms, you are in for a very good time.

Humor. Has anyone ever come up with a wholly satisfying definition of what it is? Isn't it another case of a thing that can't ever be fully defined, but as Justice Potter Stewart famously said about pornography, "I know it when I see it?" (Some don't, of course, but that's another matter.)

The great comedian, urbane wit, and humor writer Fred Allen (sorry, youngsters) may have, at the typewriter over his radio years, turned out more fine comedy in both quality and quantity than anyone who ever lived. A wit said about him, "Fred is the only man who's written more comedy material than he can lift."

"Lift" in its twin senses of "heft," of course, and also "filch." See Milton Berle. (Berle? Use Google again, kids. I have limited space.) The great comedy writer Goodman Ace called Berle "The Thief of Bad Gags."

Perhaps because Fred Allen had played not only Nebraska

but all of the West in vaudeville, much of his humor was small town and distinctly rural, as in the priceless: "It was so windy, I saw a hen lay the same egg twice."

Allen described a little New England seacoast town as so dull "that one day the tide went out . . . and never came back."

A farmer friend, Allen said, had constructed a scarecrow so terrifying "that the crows brought back corn they had stolen the year before."

What, I hear you cry, does all this have to do with Roger Welsch? It's humor, and Welsch is one of our chief practitioners, guardians, and purveyors of it.

This voluminously prolific pounder of keys has published forty-four books. This one is a book that no one on earth could have done so well. Fact, not an opinion.

Plains humor. A vast, uncharted sea of wildly funny matter that has long cried out (can a sea cry, grammarians?) for such masterful treatment. And what gems lie scattered in the bottom of that sea.

You are warned right now that this is not a joke book. If your idea of funny is, "A priest walks into a bar with a parrot on his shoulder . . . ," you're in the wrong place, my friend.

This is genuine humor of a rare and particular sensibility. As with the bar-and-parrot type of joke, the last line will, naturally, be the funny one. But the resemblance ends there. Rather than struggle further to define what's different about this treasury of laugh-out-loud and deliciously bawdy "material" that Roger has amassed and preserved, how about an example?

"I was driving the gravel to St. Paul a couple days ago and saw Kenny out on a tractor pulling a harrow. I was kind of curious because I noticed as he turned at the road end of the furrow that he was sitting on that tractor stark naked from the waist down."

Listeners at the table share expressions of wonderment.

"Yeah, I'd say so! I waited until he came back across the field and waved him down. I asked, 'What was that all about, no pants . . . half naked like that?' Kenny said, 'I worked out here all day yesterday without a shirt on and came home with a stiff neck. This,' he continues while pointing down to his absent pants, 'was my wife's idea.'"

The structural perfection and subtlety of that deceptively offhand-sounding jewel of a story merits comparison with The Greats. Really, is there anything downright funnier in Mark Twain, Noël Coward, or, yes, Oscar Wilde?

To the person sitting in darkness who'd assert that I've just besmirched great humorists by listing them with folks you might consider backwoods boobs, you are—and I mean this in the nicest way—full of something rural people are familiar with. For proof, open the book anywhere.

By the way, I'm not ashamed to report that in many cases the subtlety of these jests is of so high an order that even I—and it takes a real man to admit this—have taken a beat or two before fully getting it. I needed an instant to take in the phrase, "This was my wife's idea."

It's not that no one has covered rural, rustic, or what's mistakenly dismissed as "hayseed" humor before, but *Why I'm an Only Child and Other Slightly Naughty Plains Folktales* will surely stand as the subject's most affectionate and definitive treatment.

Again you don't find what comedy writers call hard jokes here. What's here is more like listening to good, congenial conversation. And then, without warning, you are gobsmacked with a bolt of laughter. For my money, it's because of this unexpected, sudden surprise springing from its seemingly mundane surrounding that sets this humor apart so deliciously from gags and jokes.

Not that there's anything wrong with gags and well-made jokes. Nothing wrong with, "She's so fat, when she steps on a scale, a card comes out saying, 'Please, one at a time.'" But that's not what you have here. You have something finer. More, for want of a better word, real.

Much of this great stuff sprang from one of Roger's best source locales, the venerable Dannebrog Tavern, a place I am proud to have frequented, quaffing there the best draft root beer on the planet.

Roger reports that when a colorful gang of congenial gatherers takes its place around this less cosmopolitan version of the Algonquin Round Table, no one ever says, "Okay. Time to start telling the jokes."

It's not like that. It's unplanned talk that just happens to explode now and then in a robust belly laugh. It's a little like a bunch of guys chatting and uneventfully shucking oysters when, suddenly, a pearl! The wit and humor just seem to arise as part of the fabric of conversation, whichever way it may wander. (Sorry. Now we have a wandering fabric.)

I often think of the many great things Groucho Marx said daily in conversation over the decades of his life. Words that convulsed the lucky hearers but then evaporated, unrecalled and unrecorded. Similarly I'm sure Roger hates to think how many stories—perfect candidates for this book—dissolved into thin air because no one was on duty with a good memory and a notebook.

Among related works, Vance Randolph published a collection of obscene folktales from the Ozarks with the lyrical title *Pissing in the Snow and Other Ozark Folktales.* I can't help wondering if the title relates to an oft-repeated and cherished joke of my Nebraska schoolteacher-father's. It involved that thing boys will always enjoy doing in the snow. (The punch line: "But it was in *her* handwriting.")

And note this: This funny stuff has the unique quality of being tellable in front of children and your elderly, church-going aunt Esther. Why? Because it does its magic absolutely free of dirty words. The pure in heart are safe from shock. Roger reports that that lack of filthy words protected his mother as she heard these items. Kept her free from shock. And perhaps from getting the joke.

Alas, it seems almost certain, with the inevitable changing nature of our world and its alleged sophistication, that this priceless school of humor will fade and pass from the scene, becoming one more lamented thing of the past.

It will be a major cultural loss if men with un-sunburned foreheads who live in a world of tractors, farms, crops, cows, pigs, sheep, horses, dogs, coyotes, mountain lion tracks, OshKosh B'gosh–style overalls, heavy-duty tools, anvils, and battles with savage weather no longer quaff root beer and sturdier beverages in the taverns of small-town and rural America, producing humor of the kind heroically rescued in this book.

As the rough miners out west cheered and were enchanted by the visiting aesthete Oscar Wilde, there's no reason to think the Dannebrog table would not have welcomed him too. Although Wilde worked in strikingly different forms of humor, is there any reason to assume that the Dannebrog guys wouldn't have laughed robustly at, say, Oscar's comment upon seeing Niagara Falls: "Probably the *second* great disappointment in the life of an American bride."

If Plains humor, with its limited life expectancy, must inevitably fade from the western plains like the buffalo herds of yore, all the more reason that Roger Welsch, in performing this act of preservation, should—as he would be in civilized Japan—be declared a Living National Treasure.

A word to the wise, when reading: take care not to have a mouthful of food or hot beverage when the punch line draws near.

Anyway, all that aside, just get comfortable and enjoy this book. If you have tears of laughter, prepare to shed them now.

Acknowledgments

A special acknowledgment and word of thanks to my old friend Dennis Maun who generously plowed through the early drafts of this book, always showing patience and a sense of humor even when I was pretty much sick and tired of the whole damned thing. Okay, sure, I promised him a bottle of good whiskey in return for his contribution, but no amount of whiskey of any quality can repay that kind of friendship. Thanks once again, Dennis. See you soon at Man School.

I am grateful too to my favorite son and prize-winning journalist, Chris Welsch, for helping with the copyediting of this book, one of the most important and (for me) most difficult of the processes that are an essential part of any book.

Why I'm an Only Child and Other Slightly Naughty Plains Folktales

A Brief but Suitably Scholarly and Boring Introduction

Early in my tenure in Dannebrog, Nebraska, the mail carrier Bumps Nielsen told me one of my favorite stories in this collection. As you will learn when I finally get down to sharing these delightfully risqué stories with you, they are often related in the normal course and flow of conversation; so while Bumps told me the story, he pointed at the very house where the story allegedly took place, giving his narrative an aura of truth. He said that two little boys in our town had once grown curious about conversations the big boys were having about what went on at Fifi's place (I have changed the name to protect the guilty) that cost $10. Being bright and resourceful, the boys decided to work that summer and earn enough money so that they could find out for themselves. So they mowed lawns, ran errands, scrimped, and saved, but at the end of the summer they found that they had only managed to save up $7.37. They decided, however, that with school coming on, they'd better make their move anyway; so they gathered their courage, went up the front steps to Fifi's door, and knocked.

When she answered and asked them what they wanted, one boy (again Bumps provided the name of a contemporary he knew I knew) held out a hand with their entire treasury in it and said, "Miss Fifi, we aren't sure why we're here, but we want whatever it is the big boys come here for, and we have this seven dollars and thirty-seven cents." Fifi looked those boys up and down, took the money, grabbed each of them by one ear, and banged their heads together three times just as hard as she could. Then for good measure, she threw them over the railing of the porch and out into the dust of the street. After a moment spent gathering his wits, one boy sat up, looked at the other, and opined, "I don't know about you, but I don't believe I'm ready for ten dollars' worth of that."

I feel obligated right here on the first pages of this book to do my professorial duty of defining some terms and explaining what I think is going on in the narratives I have collected over the years and now want to bring to print. And I have the feeling that by the time I am done, even though I intend to be as brief and plainspoken as I can be, you are going to be saying to yourself, "I don't know about you, but I don't believe I'm ready for ten dollars' worth of that." Well, here goes anyway. If you really don't care about the scholarly details and would just as soon skip ahead to the meatier parts of the book, I understand.

In 1976 Ozark folklorist Vance Randolph caused a considerable stir within the circle of folklore scholars and the public in general when he published his important collection of ribald folktales *Pissing in the Snow and Other Ozark Folktales* (University of Illinois Press), with an important introduction by my old friend and colleague Rayna Green. Many people, even those within the field of folklore who should have known better, were taken aback by the overt obscenity and indelicate content and language of Randolph's tales, perhaps still thinking, even after reading the unexpurgated versions of the Grimm brothers' fairy tales, that folktales should be the stuff of bedtime and kindergarten readings. Randolph's genuinely obscene stories were of the sort seldom seen in academic and, to some degree at the time, even popular publications. The language was rough and the details of the stories downright raunchy. The title refers to one of the tales in the collection, about a man complaining to his friend that the friend's son had visited and written in the snow outside his door. When the listener agreed his son was in the wrong, but noted that the prank wasn't really all so offensive, the first man responded, "There was two sets of tracks! And besides, don't you think I know my own daughter's handwriting?" It was therefore important that the introduction to *Pissing in the Snow* was written by a woman (albeit a robust woman!), thus proving, I guess, that the constitution of "the gentler sex" could bear up under the assault of depictions of explicit sex and the generally offensive language used to describe such indecencies!

My collection of ribald humor is not at all the same as Randolph's. The language and content are not nearly as rough, reflecting not at all my moral standards but, as I will explain, the sense of propriety of the people who told me these tales. These stories are not nearly as thoroughly documented as Randolph's texts because I consider them to be folklore, or the intellectual property of a societal class and not of individuals. The storytellers' names and other particulars are therefore, again in my opinion and probably not in that of more meticulous or pedantic folklore scholars, of little importance.

Moreover, because the material is—well, uh—"sensitive," I can imagine that many of my sources would prefer not to be identified. The language in the following pages is not as blunt or coarse as that found in Randolph's stories, not because of any prudery on my part but because that is the very nature of the materials I discuss here. Yes, the stories border on the ribald, although remarkably subtly; yet they are at the same time "civil." That is, they are fit for general company either because the language is seemly or because the subject is so obscured that those for whom the stories are not suitable are unlikely to understand what they are about. But still the innuendo is there, subtle or not.

I note that my stories have few analogues in Randolph's

book; the mere lack of overlap suggests to me that there are significant differences between his geographic-specific corpus and mine. That is, while the stories are somewhat alike in their sexual, social, scatological, and other content, they are most assuredly not the same narratives and, for that matter, do not take the same form. One of the reasons I have written this book is that I believe civil ribaldry is a distinctive form; although related to other folktales, jokes, off-color or offensive material, and so on, the overlap is quite narrow, and the form is distinctive.

Yet those of us who work in the field with folklore materials know that such is indeed the nature of the common stories of the common man. And of the common woman. My German great-aunts were as prim and proper a lot as you can imagine. I don't think it would be an overstatement to say they were "prudish." My mother was considered something of a rebel because—and I am not joking here—she broke with tradition by not scrubbing her sidewalks every day, and (mercy!) she scandalized her North Lincoln German family by marrying a lad from a *South* Lincoln German family. One of these stodgy, fearsome Fraus once told me in hushed tones about the time she was cleaning my cousin's room in the attic of her modest home when she found—brace yourself for the indescribable evil of it!—a deck of cards. "The Devil's handbook," she said. She marched down two flights of stairs to the basement, grabbed a small coal shovel and scuttle, went back up to the attic, scooped up the repellent object, went back down to the basement, and pitched the offending cardboards into the furnace. As she leaned forward and stared intently into my eyes, she told me that she immediately smelled the distinctive reek of brimstone.

And yet in that same year at a wedding dance I saw that stout little lady join the other proper women of the family who gathered at the front of the hall, where the bride and groom sat in chairs. The women regaled the couple with *tusch* (toasts) to their marital happiness. But their tusch were not just toasts of congratulations and best wishes. No, these traditional quatrains spoke lasciviously of *gummer* (cucumbers) and *wascht* (sausages), sometimes accompanied with illustrative gestures. The crowd roared, the bride blushed, the groom grinned, and more and more of these staid aunts of mine stepped forward to offer their own metaphors of . . .

Of . . . what? The obscene? How can things as mundane as foodstuffs be considered obscene? There was no dirty language here. Nothing as evil as a deck of cards. Just rhymes about what the bride and groom might enjoy over the coming days and years. What could be more innocent? And where could these toasts be more at home than in peasant circles, where earthiness was not just tolerated but celebrated? All the while within these same circles, genuine obscenity such as coarse language was *never* to be found. (My mother's strongest curse was "Gewitter [thunderstorms]!") And these were women, after all. You know, the gentler, more sensitive gender. (I almost wrote "sex," but my aunts and mother would never have approved of that word!) Men like to think that they are the only ones who speak the unspeakable, but women know otherwise.

Obscenity is an indeterminate quality. It varies with the context in which it appears, with the language in which it is couched, with time and geography. Jokes that might be tolerated in the city are out of place in the country, while ribald narratives laughed at in a rural context might even go unnoticed by city slickers, as I discuss in the following stories. My daughter Antonia has scolded me for language that I consider innocent enough but that has become inappropriate for her generation; similarly, words she tosses about with no particular embarrassment leave me shocked and wide eyed.

Despite the common misunderstanding, laughter is not

the universal language. My wife Linda and I share a common sense of humor, and it has been there from the beginning and is not a product of our long years together. Meanwhile, words and stories *have* resulted from those decades that are funny only to us and not even to our own children. My best friend, Mick, and I also find some of our stories to be hilariously funny while Linda thinks they are too adolescent to be considered interesting, let alone funny. In the same vein, while Americans consider extreme violence to be perfectly acceptable fare for the big screen or even the family television set, they shrink away from nudity and sex, which people in other parts of the world find as natural as the passing of the seasons. Many cultures consider greed and selfishness to be the worst of all sins, but in this country they are celebrated as "evidence of the success of the free market."

In fact, a double standard seems to be *the* standard in cultural matters. Or maybe it should be a triple or even quadruple standard. Sometimes the very same materials are both acceptable and unacceptable within the exact same group. William Hugh Jansen, another friend and folklorist colleague of mine, formulated what he dubbed the "es-ex factor." There is a dynamic of esoteric and exoteric contexts: is the material in question being used within a closed group (esoterically) or outside the group (exoterically)? As with so many traditional things, these dynamics are not even detected in many cases, let alone understood. People who should be able to figure it out on their own nonetheless express confusion and maybe even indignation that black singers, athletes, or co-workers can use what we delicately tiptoe around by referring to as "the N-word" but then take offense when the term is used outside their own racial circles. There it is . . . the es-ex factor. I now find myself enough of an insider that I can joke with my Czech in-laws about their being bohunks, a term that is pejorative when used by someone not "in the circle," and exchange inside jokes about tribal issues and characteristics with my Indian family and friends. But in fact I still exercise caution when indulging in insider humor. While I can use some language and tell some jokes when I am in the company of members of those very same societies that are the butts of the jokes and language, telling them outside those circles would be seen not as a sign of acceptance both of me in those circles and of those circles in my life but rather as an insult directed at those groups.

Moreover, as I discuss in the following section, using such language and telling tales (or jokes) in the right way and within appropriate contexts make them not insults at all but a way of appropriating and disarming insults. Nothing stops ugliness faster than laughter. As a quick survey of my published works shows, I have always enjoyed humor and sharing with others what I discover in my folklore studies. In this volume I certainly look forward to sharing with you readers the laughter I have found in these stories. At the same time, as I believe this genre of folktale has received little notice before, I hope to make a contribution to folklore studies by bringing the field's attention to what I have chosen to call civil ribaldry. I do so because I think the subtlety and polish of the materials says a lot about the elegant quality of the traditional tale.

And the following are by and large *tales*. They are narratives. They tell a story. They are not the same as the modern joke, which may take the form of a riddle or a one-liner or simply a wisecrack (although I do include examples of this abbreviated gag-line humor throughout the book to illustrate various points). Most of the stories I discuss in these pages have plots, even as terse and as simple as they may be. And they are folklore. That is, they are not generally materials that are invented by a single creative mind but are circulated, usually orally, from one person to another. And they are not done so in print or in a performance format or on a stage or in front of a camera but around tavern tables, at family picnics, around campfires, or in an office lunchroom.

I am eager to get on with the storytelling, yet I also want to tell you about how I collected the stories, why I included these stories here and not others, what I left out, and where and how the stories are told. Actually some of these details about the nature of the collection and the process of collecting will almost certainly be clearer to you, the reader, once you have . . . well . . . read the book. So at this point I am going to launch into the materials themselves, and at the end of the book, if you are patient and if you wish, you can find further particulars in the afterword.

But Enough about Me—
What Do *You* Know about Me?

It's not common that an author thanks the publisher of his book. For one thing, the relationship between the two is not always as congenial as mine has been over the years with the University of Nebraska Press. Don't get me wrong: The press and I have had our disagreements about spellings, book design, and even cover art. I recall rather clearly standing on Bill Regier's front porch and screaming obscenities after seeing the new design for the press's edition of *Catfish at the Pump: Humor and the Frontier.* Bill had rejected my wife Linda's design, which was used for the first edition of the book, because it was a line drawing and was yellow. As I saw when I opened the package, the press's new edition was . . . yellow. And it featured a line drawing . . . that had absolutely nothing to do with the content of the book. (As it turned out, the design came from a contracting artist in Texas who had not bothered to read the book!) I was livid.

But I got over it. And small wonder, because my relationship with the University of Nebraska Press has lasted longer and has been more cordial than a lot of marriages. Ten of my forty-four books have now found a home with the press. That is important to me not simply because every writer wants his books to find a home—any home!—but also because it is an organ of the University of Nebraska. Somewhere in my closet I have a cape that a fan and friend made for me that has CAPTAIN NEBRASKA emblazoned on it. My license plates used to say CAPTNEB. And I still consider myself to be a particularly zealous advocate of this state, which a journalist from Texas, of all places, has called "a hulking giant" and which its own citizens have denigrated as a place that has nothing to offer but football. (Look out, Captain! He's about to blow!)

My father shoveled coal from railcars into the maw of the university's powerhouse when he was sixteen and the powerhouse stood at the south end of what is now Memorial Stadium. (Later he worked his way up to janitor—*up* to janitor [consider that for a moment]—to fireman, then to stationary steam engineer.) I earned two degrees from the university and was granted an honorary degree from the university's Kearney campus. I taught at the Lincoln campus as a graduate teaching assistant. Much later I became a faculty member in the University of Nebraska's English and Anthropology Departments, a fellow of the Center for Great Plains Studies, a fellow of the university's Centennial Education Program, a recipient of distinguished teaching awards, a member of the graduate faculty, an adviser to the school's boxing club for a decade, and eventually a full professor with tenure. My son Chris graduated from the university, was editor of the *Daily Nebraskan*, played on the school's rugby team, and even more heroically attended the club's physically demanding after-game parties. My daughter Joyce graduated with honors in the Theater Department and went on to become a distinguished attorney. My granddaughter Jacinda also attended classes at the university. I met my beloved wife Linda there when she was a secretary in the Education Department. She made the mistake of taking advantage of the school's perk of letting staff take one class per semester, and she chose to take a class in folklore from the English Department's Mad Man in Overalls. To this day I am a ferocious advocate of the University of Nebraska as an educational and research institution, not a source of silly Saturday afternoon amusements.

The University of Nebraska. The University of Nebraska Press. I don't think anyone has been more strongly affected by those institutions than I have been. But the moment that comes to my mind at this point is the day in 1964 when I walked into the offices of the University of Nebraska Press, housed in Lincoln's old Elgin Watch Factory at Sixteenth and X Streets, with a typewritten manuscript in my hands. I said to Bruce Nicoll, "Uh . . . I wrote this book. It's about Nebraska folklore. And, well, I was wondering if maybe you'd want to publish it?"

I had already written a few minor articles for publication, most of which dealt with folklore, specifically Nebraska folklore. I was taking graduate courses in the Folklore Institute at Indiana University and earning some extra money and getting in stolen study moments while working in the institute's library. I was cleaning books and shelves one summer day in 1963 when I came upon a row of books, which were just barely books since they were only bound mimeographed sheets, labeled "Nebraska Folklore." Wow. At that time it had never occurred to me that there was such a thing as Nebraska folklore. I was playing in coffeehouses, singing British whaling songs and Irish ballads, and trying my best to imitate the folk singer Pete Seeger, Huddie "Lead Belly" Ledbetter, Burl Ives, and Harry Belafonte, but . . . There is *Nebraska* folklore?

And there it was. I thought I'd had an epiphany when I discovered the idea of folklore as an alternative to high art and culture, but now . . . folklore from Nebraska? Really? I devoured those bound pamphlets. And used my bottom-of-the-ladder academic position to check out the volumes long enough to take them back to Nebraska and hand copy them. I read the stories word for word. I learned the songs and almost immediately did an LP vinyl recording of some of those songs for the Smithsonian Folkways Records in 1966 that is still in distribution as a CD by the Library of Congress American Folklife Center. Nebraska folklore . . . who would have guessed? From there I sought out Nebraska tall tales (again inspired by the Federal Writers' Project [FWP] materials from the Work Projects Administration that I found in those mimeographed pamphlets) and a book about horse traders . . . Same story. All are now in publication by the University of Nebraska Press.

That's how a life seems to go, at least from my own experience. Again I've retold them in more recent UNP publications—*Embracing Frybread: Confessions of a Wannabe* and *The Reluctant Pilgrim: A Skeptic's Journey into Native Mysteries.* (That's right; there were FWP pamphlets in the Nebraska collection about Native American stories too!)

Now here I am again, manuscript in hand, but fifty glorious years and more than forty books and thousands of articles later. And that's why this slim volume of modestly ribald tales—this time collected by me rather than by the noble and remarkably talented FWP collectors of the late 1930s—is so important to me. I wonder if any other scholar has published over so many years with the University of Nebraska Press. (I'm certain that some authors have placed more books with the press; certainly my old friend and colleague Paul Johnsgard has outstripped me in that category.) Perhaps then you can imagine what this volume means to me. I no longer need entries in my bibliography to gain academic tenure, promotion, or approval. I no longer have to worry about propriety. I live on a bare minimum, but that's okay because I don't need anything more. Linda and I have returned our only home and property to the Pawnee Nation. During my years with CBS News doing my "Postcards from Nebraska" for *CBS Sunday Morning,* Charles Kuralt taught me how to ignore distracters.

In all honesty, after all these years in folklore and Nebraska, I'm still not convinced that there is a *Nebraska* folklore, a body of traditional materials that are exclusively or even primarily Nebraskan. No, I am sure there is *not* such a thing. Nebraska lies at the heart of the Continent, at the center of the Great Plains. That means it is the crossroads for many traditions converging from all the edges and corners. Even while there are still Native tribes such as the Omahas, who have been here for centuries, there have been massive inflows of immigrant peoples, each group with its own traditional lore.

And each has its own sense of humor. In moments when I am honest with myself and I think about this matter of a *Nebraska* folklore, I confess quietly my suspicions that the work I have done in this state and in this field of study all my life really means that I have discovered only Roger's folklore . . . the things I have been interested in: sod houses, dogs, Indians, folksongs, outhouses and barns, wild foods, old tractors, and above and before all else, *humor.* I love laughter. It's one of the main reasons I became interested in Indians and fell in love with Linda. Humor is in large part how I choose my friends. And it has again and again led me to areas I want to know more about: the tall tale, the exaggeration postcard, horse-trading stories, and now, here, the ribald story, which is all the more interesting to me because it has the added surprise and asset of subtlety. I enjoy a raunchy joke as much as the next guy, but even more I enjoy these stories I have come to know as civil ribaldry precisely because they walk the narrow line between being obscene and socially acceptable. Are these stories exclusively Nebraskan or even Plains or geographically specific at all? I can't really argue that, nor am I interested in the idea. I do have the feeling, as I did with my tall-tale studies, that however widely distributed through time and geography the genre is, it seems to have found a particularly suitable soil here in the Central Plains. As with the tall tale, I believe these gentle if evocative bits of humor reflect directly the personality of the people of the Plains and therefore of Nebraska.

So I offer up the wonderful tales of this collection as a tribute to all those from whom they came: to *real* Nebraskans, to my peasant kin and kind, to a long and wonderful life of discovery and wonder, to the Plains geography I love from the bottom of my heart, to the very idea of folklore, to Indians and pioneers I know and love, to the friends I've known around campfires and in rural taverns, and to anyone not afraid to laugh, even when the story told is at the edge of propriety.

Plain Talk about the Plains, Definitions, and What Folklore Is, Isn't, Might Be, and Is Mostly

It's easy enough to figure out what is and isn't Nebraska. I mean, there it is in my road atlas between Montana and Nevada. You might confuse one rectangular state for another—Colorado for Wyoming, for instance—but there's no mistaking the distinctive shape of Nebraska. And yet except for the formidable eastern boundary of the state, formed by the Missouri River, there's nothing at all distinct about the landscape of the Great Plains as the geography shifts from Nebraska into Kansas or South Dakota.

I was only six or seven years old when my mother and I took a passenger train west from Lincoln to visit relatives in Wyoming. I remember alternately looking at a map of the United States that I had from school and peering out the window as we passed through town after town, hoping to see the precise place where, as shown on the map, Nebraska's light yellow turned into Wyoming's pink. I discovered quickly that while the geography did indeed change, from what I would later learn is the tallgrass prairie to the short-grass prairie and then to the only sparsely grassed high plains, the lines and colors on the map are arbitrary concepts devised by politicians, delineated by surveyors, and presented by cartographers and printers. There are no such lines. There are short-grass prairies, tallgrass prairies, high plains, foothills, and mountains, but the lines do not exist. The real geographies fade inexorably one into the other.

Culture is like that. So is language. And time. We use

specific words like "art," "English," and "times like these," but the reality is not so clear as the words suggest or as they come to be understood. There are centers where such concepts are strongest and most obvious, but as we move toward the edges, things are not as clear. In fact, they can become downright confusing. I have seriously explored the concept of "folklore" for almost sixty-five years, or about as long as anyone living has, I imagine. So by now I'm fairly confident that I know what folklore, or folk art, or folktales are; what traditionally transmitted materials are; what popular culture is; and what fine art is, as surely as I know that here at the edge of the Nebraska Sandhills I live on the Great Plains. But trying to tell someone else what the character and nature of such amorphous ideas are . . . that is a much harder task. Some people take the easy route and offer up charts, maps, lists, categories, or simply words—"Great Plains," "folklore." That won't work, however, when one is faced with actual situations and items. "How about here, Rog? Is this grassy hill just west of Lincoln part of the prairie or the Plains? Is this spring, or is it now summer? Is this song folklore or popular culture? Or what exactly is it?"

Well, such things aren't exact. But I can provide some general descriptions of what we can look for, even though there are no boundaries between such concepts, and given a bit of time, one thing is likely to change inexorably into another. That is, not only are such ideas vague to begin with, they are constantly in flux, growing or diminishing, changing, becoming something else, perhaps dying altogether. Some people are frustrated by such uncertainty; I am exhilarated by it. So it is with folklore and, in the case of this book, the folklore in general and the specific subcategory of folktale I call civil ribaldry.

It doesn't help at all that some words such as "folklore" are used in many different ways by different people and sometimes in different ways by the same person in different contexts. *Folklorists*, people who work professionally with traditional materials, use the word "folklore" with a fairly restricted meaning, excluding a lot of things others might think of as folklore and including some things that might surprise people who are not seriously concerned with traditional culture. When I taught folklore classes, I first listed some of the common perceptions the general public had about folklore that those of us who look at such materials seriously do not understand to be a part of it. On the one hand, for example, the word "folklore" is commonly used in general conversation to designate something that is simply wrong or false: "The Fact, Fiction, and Folklore of Cancer." It's not that such usage is incorrect, but when I am speaking or writing about folklore, I do not use it in that sense. The fact of the matter is, in my experiences folklore is remarkably accurate and true, coming as it does out of generations, even centuries, of experience and observation. An Omaha Indian friend once told me while we were out in the country, well away from medical supplies, that I might find relief from my headache by chewing on a willow stick. Later I learned that the scientific name for willow is "salix," and the inner bark contains salicin, which metabolizes into salicylic acid. That is . . . aspirin! The advice I got was an item of folk medicine . . . and as true as any science.

On the other hand, folklore is not always true. It depends, I guess, on whether it's true or not! The point is, whether it's true or not has nothing to do with whether it is folklore or not. Some folklore—quilting, much of folk music, folk dance—is beautiful; some expressions, such as racism, gender oppression, religious extremism, aren't. Folklore also is not necessarily old. I'd bet I could sit down with you right now and in a matter of minutes find folklore in your own life, no matter who you are or what you do. It may not be the same tradition, a word that is often used for folklore, as your grandfather's or grandmother's—in fact, it may be grounded in very new forms or bases—but it's there. And it's alive and dynamic. Folklore that is common in one place or at one time may fade away over time, new forms of folklore may grow or move from one group to another, and sometimes a form of folklore simply changes. A song from black prison lore, like "Goodnight, Irene," may find its way into a circle of Girl Scouts around a campfire. "Goodnight, Irene," which musicologists John Lomax and Alan Lomax recorded Lead Belly singing a month before his release from the Louisiana State Prison in 1934, was popularized in 1950 by the Weavers after cleaning up some of the racier lyrics. For example, the line "I gets you in my dreams" was changed to the version that scouts around the campfire sing today: "I'll *see* you in my dreams."

Speaking of Lead Belly's prison song "Goodnight, Irene," I am reminded of another situation where I was faced with the task of identifying musicians in German communities in America (already confusing!) who were genuinely part of a community tradition and not engaged in what professional folklorists sometimes label "folklorico," or performance arts that are developed and presented primarily for audiences that are not part of the community. In other words, they are tourist or promotional forms that are presented as but are not in reality authentic elements of the community. It wouldn't have done me any good to ask the musicians if they were indeed authentic, because they would have insisted they were, and to the extent that we are all authentically *some*thing, yes, they were! To some degree I could watch a performance and judge its authenticity, for example, by their costuming. People who are really part of a community dress as other members of the community do; even if they're in clothing meant for special occasions, the musicians are not authentic if that clothing is worn *only* during performances.

But the touchstone I found most useful was to ask the

musicians to play what they played at the last wedding in the community. Those engaged in folklorico are not usually asked to perform for weddings because their performances are meant for the outside world. Moreover, genuine folklore is largely done unself-consciously. That is, the people who participate in it view it simply as . . . what is done. Not something extraordinary or peculiar but just another part of normal life. One of the finest craftsmen and musicians I knew in those days when I was working for the Smithsonian Institution's Folklife Festival on the Mall celebrations was Albert Fahlbusch, a master hammered dulcimer player and maker in the German Russian community of Scottsbluff, Nebraska. That evaluation was not mine alone; the National Endowment for the Arts awarded him a fellowship in 1984. Early in our contacts I attended a couple of wedding dances where Albert; his son, Roger; and other musicians performed as a group. I heard them play what they played at weddings, music known and appreciated in their German community: "Der Hinkel un' die Ginkel (The Rooster and the Hen)," an age-old, traditional dance tune from the German communities that once filled the Volga River Valley north of the Black Sea; "Blue Skirt Waltz," a recorded success of Frankie Yankovic's in 1949 and then later a television standard of Lawrence Welk's band; and then, to my delight, "Goodnight, Irene."

Okay, what's the apple-cheeked, well-intentioned folklorist to make of this set? Are these songs folksongs? Is "Der Hinkel un' die Ginkel" compromised by being performed in Scottsbluff, Nebraska, rather than in Schaefer, Russia? On amplified instruments? What is one to make of the cultural clash of Lawrence Welk in the same repertoire as Lead Belly? One could pick at the individual constituents of that night's performance, but what I saw was a community celebrating its traditions. Although it was no longer a three-day wedding dance, which was still practiced when I was child in a German community like Albert Fahlbusch's, and a lot more English than German was spoken (and sung), and a lot of German food was served but washed down with another translated and transmuted Teutonic tradition, Budweiser beer, what was important to me was that Fahlbusch's group made no effort here to be "authentic" because everything in the total matrix of the dance *was* authentic. Because that's what one did in Scottsbluff at a German Russian wedding. Not by order of a wedding planner or rules of the state or edicts of the church. Things were simply done the traditional way such things were done. And everyone knew how such things were done.

I once asked Albert how he should be identified when I spoke about him to my supervisors at the Smithsonian. His response was telling: he looked at me blankly. I asked again. He said, confused, "Truck driver." I asked again. He said, "Nebraskan." We continued down the same line: "German Russian." "Lutheran." "Husband." At no point did it occur to him to respond, "Folk musician." He probably had never heard the term until he saw himself so identified on a program in Washington DC. He didn't have to try to be anything because he was what he was. And he was a master musician, a craftsman, and a genuine item of folklore, an unself-conscious but crucial element of his community.

The individual elements of Albert's repertoire, or of the celebrants' food or language or drinks, would be of little consequence in determining his authenticity—unless one's intention was to examine those items. Even then the judgments would be difficult. If I were cornered and threatened with something terrible like three hours of watching Home and Garden Television, I'd say, "Okay, 'Der Hinkel un' die Ginkel' . . . clearly a folksong. Even when played on a hammered dulcimer with an electronic pickup. 'Blue Skirt Waltz,' as an item, popular culture, but maybe . . . here . . . hard to say. 'Goodnight, Irene,' in its bowdlerized form, transmitted to Albert Fahlbusch and the Polka Playboys . . . Draw me another mug of beer from the keg, give me one more dance with the bride, and I'll get back to you on that one."

Individual items of folklore may be old, are almost always passed from one person to another, and are often fairly simple, even basic, but that doesn't mean the folklore is primitive. It is, in fact, a demanding, high aesthetic. If you don't believe me, try it for yourself. I have watched people who think the sod house or the log house would be easy to replicate, since it is, after all, "primitive." They learn quickly and inevitably that such folk architecture is in fact precise, complicated, and utilitarian and that naive efforts without the required knowledge lead to failure. Those old-timers knew what they were doing. So do Native American beadworkers.

I can imagine too that some readers might be surprised to find log construction and beadwork included in the category of folklore. In fact, folklore is much larger than the most widely understood categories of folksong and folktale, and it includes other traditional skills such as folk architecture, foodways, medicine, speech, poetry, custom, costume, dance, crafts, history, law, and on and on. In fact, if you were to take a university catalog of class offerings, you could go right down the list and find that a parallel body of knowledge is transmitted and held within folkloric tradition. Sometimes the very ideas that have been born or maintained within the informal transmission of tradition find their way into formal culture too. One cannot study William Shakespeare without considering the folklore he constantly incorporated into his classic works. No study of theology is complete without thinking of the traditionally held aspects of faith. What could be more academic and couched in formality than law? And yet in my own experience, sometimes with dismay, I have heard a judge say, "Well, Mr. Welsch, that is indeed how the law reads and what the law says. But that is not the way we do it here."

In a crunch, when someone *demands* a definition of "folklore," and when I don't have the luxury or inclination to belabor the poor interrogator with all the words I have now thrown at you in saying what folklore isn't (but *may* be!) and sometimes is (but not *always*!), niggling about problems of definitions and providing analogies and metaphors, example and errors, I wind up reciting something like this: "Folklore is that part of culture that is transmitted primarily from person to person by informal means . . . word of mouth, example, demonstration, daily activity . . . rather than through formal conduits of knowledge like classrooms, books, galleries, or concert halls." Then I move quickly closer to the bar and strike up a conversation with folks who look as though they are already deep enough in their cups that they won't be asking me any hard questions.

It's one thing to deal with all this in the abstract, but, man, it sure gets complicated when dealing with the larger body of culture in the field. If the task is to collect and analyze one specific form of folklore—proverbs, folk rhymes, riddling jokes, urban legends, insult rhymes, mnemonic devices, incantations, curses—where does one start, and where does one end? One of the issues I have tried to deal with in my study is to sort out this one particular form of humorous, traditional tale that in its natural form lives in a huge matrix of other folktale forms—oral history, legend, joke, and personal anecdote—and many of which are also humorous. But many of which are not folklore. At what point, if ever, does one person's or one family's story about a disastrous Christmas dinner, perhaps the time Uncle Ned was thoroughly sloshed by the time he was scheduled to be the evening's Santa, become folklore?

It doesn't help that unlike some folktale forms, there are no overt indicators when someone is about to tell one of the stories I call civil ribaldry. The fairy tale, now largely dead within Western folklore and only told on the large screen by Pixar or Walt Disney Studios, always had a clear opening and closing when it existed in oral tradition—"once upon a time . . ." and "they lived happily ever after"—and contained obvious elements that identified it as a fairy tale: things happening in threes, talking animals, established names such as Snow White and Sleeping Beauty. Jokes are usually told almost as if in performance, with joke tellers playing off of each other and introductory lines such as "Did you hear the one about . . . ?" Again they feature unlikely but traditional characters and elements ("a priest, a rabbi, and a Baptist minister walk into a bar . . ."). Often (but not always, as the structural elements of civil ribaldry are not hard and certain) even an appreciative audience like me has no idea he is hearing one of these delights until the subtle performance is over.

I can imagine someone in North Carolina or Oregon protesting that the stories I tell here are not Plains folktales at all because "I heard the same story here three days ago." I have identified these stories as Plains tales because I have collected them in Nebraska, in the heart of the Plains. Also I have rarely heard or seen them anywhere else. "Rarely" doesn't mean "never," but my impression—and that's all it is—is that as with my previous conclusions about the tall tale, the environment of the Plains has been especially fertile soil for this particular genre of tale. As are the Plains, the ribald tales are—again generally but not always—rural, agricultural, subtle, and civil. Not always. But usually.

So as we sort through the following stories, aside from my hope that you will find the same laughter in the stories that I have enjoyed over the years, please have sympathy with my efforts to discuss these wonderful items even as I jerk them from their natural contexts and commit the sin of talking seriously about humor. Doing so is akin to writing about philosophy in *Playboy*: you have to be careful, or readers will think you believe that's why they're reading the magazine. So there you have it: Folklore is that part of culture passed along to us informally; it is part of what makes us what we are. The stories you are about to read are one of the many types of narrative called the folktale, which is part of that huge body of traditional material called folklore.

A Lesson in Proper Diction

My father was a middle-class factory worker, son of migrant sugar beet laborers. He finished his high school education a few years before I finished mine. He was a plainspoken, unpretentious fellow, but I never heard him swear. Ever. I was well into my seniority too before my curiosity grew to the point where I decided to ask him whatever reasons there might be for this unlikely sense of propriety. There were occasions when his self-control in this regard seemed almost inappropriate to me. Once when we were working in our Victory Garden, which should give some of my older readers an idea of when this happened and how young I was, a bird—I don't know how to say this delicately—pooped on Dad's head. Since it was mulberry season, the event was even more dramatic than it might have been at any other time of the year. I stood there with my hoe, stunned, waiting for the explosion that was sure to follow. Dad slowly took a kerchief from his back pocket, wiped the offending blotch from his forehead, looked skyward, and said, quietly and to my lifelong education thereafter, "For the rich you sing."

I was well into my own seniority before I mentioned his avoidance of profanity because the implication of such a question would be that I thought it would be okay to use bad language and, since it was obvious that Dad did not, that I would be courting a lecture (usually delivered in the form of few words and with a stern look of disapproval). It simply didn't seem proper. Moreover, as I recall, I didn't ask the question; instead, I just mentioned it in passing. You know, like, "Hey, Dad. I've noticed that you never cuss. That's pretty rare these days. Especially with men." I'd guess Dad was maybe sixty years old by that time, which would mean that I was about thirty-seven. But it seemed a question worth asking because Dad was not a prude; he just didn't swear.

I'm glad I brought the issue up, however, because Dad then told me a remarkable story that explained a lot more than any notion of some kind of Puritanical restraint. For many years I had been collecting a kind of joke, or more precisely a humorous story, that seemed a trifle racy without being, well, . . . "dirty." I knew that Dad was partial to this genre, but I had always wondered about the disconnect between what seemed his almost prudish nature and his perfectly normal male taste for racy stories. Or, in his case, *slightly* racy stories.

But I'm already about to get ahead of myself in my eagerness to tell you some of these stories. I'll tell you what my father told me when I first asked about his obvious delight in ribald stories and yet with what seemed to me at the time a curious avoidance of language usually associated with Vance Randolph's materials. Dad reminded me that when he was a little boy, his parents had managed the JayEm Ranch in eastern Wyoming. You know, not far from the communities of Redbird, Dull Center, and Bill but quite a ways north of Chugwater. (Excuse me for the unnecessary detail, but one doesn't get much of a chance to write observations about Wyoming geography—more's the pity. So I have to jump at the opportunity when it arises, no matter how strained the references.)

Anyway, Dad said, he was always hanging around with the cowboys, and in the process he learned cowboy language. Dad was maybe six or seven years old when he spent his days out in the corrals and barn, loitering around the cowboys on the JayEm Ranch and enriching his vocabulary, so to speak. It was approaching noon one day when one of the cowboys observed to his colleagues that if that Chris kid used that kind of corral language when they went into the house for lunch, Mr. Welsch was not going to be happy, and that meant they would all be in trouble. Or worse yet, they would be in Dutch with Mrs. Welsch, the cook, and that is never a good place to be for the workingman. There was a good chance they would be out of a job by sundown.

So they gathered around the kid—my father, that is—and explained to him that he couldn't use the kind of language they used when they were out working around the ranch. Just couldn't do it. He'd get them all in trouble if he did. Dad, being a youngster, a German, and a Welsch, said hell no, he wouldn't shut up. In fact, he'd use any goddamn language he wanted to. And if those words were good enough for the cowboys, then it sure as shit was good enough for him.

The cowboys explained the situation again, perhaps a bit more strongly. Still Dad refused to back down. The cowboys now realized they were heading for real trouble. (I only barely knew my grandmother, being perhaps only six or seven years old when she died, but I remember her well enough to know she was not a woman to be trifled with.) One of the cowboys picked Dad up by his overall straps, pulled him up nose to nose, and told him in unmistakable terms that if he ever cussed again, there would be hell to pay. Dad defiantly returned the favor, blueing the air with barnyard language.

The cowboys were now desperate. And my grandmother was ringing the noon bell, signaling them to come in for her irresistible cooking. (Again my memories of the woman are not many, but I do remember her cooking.) It was showdown time at the JayEm corral. The cowboy who had been lecturing my father looked around for a path out of his dilemma and spotted a large nail protruding from one of the barn's support posts. Still having Dad lofted by his overall straps, he hung Dad from that nail and said, "If you don't promise me that you'll never cuss again, Chris Welsch, you're going to hang there on that nail until hell freezes over." Dad stuck out his jaw and spat out yet another curse.

So the cowboys went in to eat the noon meal, leaving Dad hanging by his overall straps on that nail. By the time they came out, Dad was ready to foreswear his bad habits and swore (in a manner of speaking) never to swear again. The cowboys took him down from his perch, he went into the house for a late meal, and he never swore again.

As I said . . . he was a German, a Welsch, and a man of his word. And that explains why I never heard my father cuss.

Eighty-some years after that hanging, moreover, Dad's sister Emma and one of my cousins went to that selfsame barn in JayEm, removed that nail, and presented it to me as one of my prized possessions in this life. I worry that some day someone will look at that rusty spike, wonder why I put it away in a nice box with my other treasures, and throw it away. That's one of the reasons, however, why I am telling the story here. Now my own children will know that old, bent bit of rust is as precious to me as if it were solid gold.

Why I'm an Only Child

Stories like the one my dad told about not swearing don't come along every day. A conversational fuse has to be lit; the right word, phrase, situation, or question is needed to jar the memory of the storyteller. The agile mind then sorts through the teller's memory banks, and there you are: just the right circumstances evoke a story, often the kind that amuses a collector of such things. Me, for instance. If I hadn't said something to my father at just the right moment, would I have ever heard Dad's cussing story? There's a good chance I wouldn't have and might never had had the privilege to know this precious gem of family history. Same with the kind of stories I deal with in this book. Dad told lots of stories after all. In fact, he seemed to specialize, once I thought about it, in mildly off-color ones. What about them? Was his aversion to swearing a reason why he seemed so attracted to them? Did he perhaps think he could get away with telling them because there were no "bad" words in them? One thing's for certain: he sure was a fount of the stories that I later came to call civil ribaldry.

On another occasion I asked him a *very* delicate personal question. I would have never ventured onto that shaky ground except that Dad opened the topic when he once said something about the reason I was an only child. Dad was struck by lightning when he was a boy and had suffered problems from that trauma all his life. He was deaf from that point on, for example, and I thought maybe it had affected him . . . well, otherwise.

But here was my chance, so I asked, "Gee, Dad, why *am* I an only child?"

He said, "Because I got a hearing aid."

Long, puzzled silence. "Because . . . you got . . . a hearing aid?"

"Yep."

"Uuuh . . . why? . . . What? . . . Uuuh . . ."

"See, Rog, when your mother and I were first married, we'd go to bed, and she would say, 'Well, Chris, do you want to just go to sleep or what?' Then I'd say, 'WHAT?' Then you were born, and I got a hearing aid."

My father told a lot of stories about being deaf because he was deaf. An important element of humor is self-deprecation. It is a defense mechanism. You don't want people to make fun of your weakness? Then laugh at it yourself, and that leaves them pretty much without ammunition. So Dad was a treasury of stories about deafness. When I started to lose my own hearing, the product of an appreciation for rock-and-roll music, he told me to forget the notion of hearing aids. He said, "Drape a piece of string over your ear and into your pocket. You won't need a hearing aid. People will see that string and talk louder."

One of his favorite stories was about a time when he was visiting an otologist about a decline in his hearing. The doctor examined him and exclaimed with some amazement, "Well, Chris, no wonder you can't hear out of this ear. There's a suppository stuck in here!" To which Dad said, "So . . . *that's* what happened to my hearing aid."

Along those same lines, I was present when Dad told a doctor that the suppositories that he had prescribed weren't "worth a darn." Dad said, "They were next to impossible to swallow, and for all the good they did me, I might as well have stuffed them up my butt." Don't bother telling me that's an old joke. That's what folklore is all about. New jokes aren't folklore. Dad wasn't inventive; he just knew a good story when he heard one. Then he stored it away in his mental inventory, and when the appropriate occasion arose, he pulled it out and delivered it much as he had heard it but perhaps with slightly better timing. That's how folklore comes to be the art it is. That is, Dad didn't do performances, announcing implicitly or overtly that he was about to tell some jokes; instead, a situation or conversation arose that set up his story, more often than not by those who were about to become his audience, and with perfect timing and no announcement, he told his story.

Somewhere along the line I realized that Dad could have told stories like the one about why I was an only child in front of a crowd of kids, and they'd have no idea what he was talking about. After all it took me a few minutes to catch on to that one myself. (Now, be honest. It took *you* a moment to get it too, didn't it?) Wow. He had told a slightly racy story, with no bad language and not even suggestive language. Almost in code. I tucked that vignette away in my mind, thinking it was more interesting than simply a personal story about my family. I'm betting he had heard something like that somewhere along the line before. Not only did my question present an occasion to use the gag, but also it was the only occasion in his life when it would be appropriate since its very nature required a dialogue between a father and an only child. And here I was, his only child. Nor have I ever heard the story told by or about anyone else. However, being a folklorist and having previously encountered unique situations where traditional stories were evoked, not to be heard by me again, I knew that while the circumstance was singular, the story probably was not. I had just been privileged to witness the one time in Dad's life when that story was the right story to tell.

A Special Announcement

As such things tend to go in storytelling traditions, I didn't have to wait long for another nudge to pay more attention to what was going on here. And I think it was the moment I realized that I *had* to write something about this remarkable genre of storytelling: Linda and I were at my parents' home in Lincoln, Nebraska, and planned to use the occasion for, gulp, a "special announcement."

By way of background, my long history of "special announcements" to my folks had established a precedent for familial trauma . . . a divorce, the adoption of a minority child, a hippie history, and my near expulsion from the family because my father did not approve of my prodigal ways: my long hair, my preference for wearing overalls rather than a coat and tie (even as a professor while teaching university classes), my weedy lawn, and then my second marriage to—gasp, choke!—a Catholic Bohemian woman eighteen years my junior. My father had cautioned me in my youth, "Roger, if you never date a Catholic girl, you'll never wind up marrying one." I dated one. I married her. So you can see why this dinner offered yet another threat of cardiac arrest for my long-suffering parents.

It was a lovely supper. Mom was a terrific cook. And over the first three years of this second marriage my parents had become very fond of Linda. I think it was about that time that Mom said, "Roger, if you ever get another divorce, we're keeping Linda and getting rid of *you*," and she wasn't joking. When we finished the meal and dessert was on the table, I cleared my throat to make a special announcement: "Mom, Dad, . . . Linda and I would like to share some special news with you." Mom groaned and dropped her head to the table. Dad put his fork to his plate, obviously waiting for the worst. Which I gave him. "Uh, . . . in September Linda and I . . . are going to have a baby."

Again, here's some personal background: By this time I already had three children from a previous marriage. The youngest was just fifteen years old; the oldest, only ten years younger than Linda. And my daughter Jennifer had already announced *she* would present me with my first grandchild in September. So my dad's reaction was going to be interesting. The silence was long and uncomfortable. In fact, at the time it seemed to go on forever. Then Dad cleared *his* throat and said, "Rog, once an old man was out walking in the woods. He encountered a bear. He raised his cane and yelled, 'BANG!' At the same time a young man was out hunting in those same woods. He too saw the bear and raised his gun and shot at the very same instant the old man raised his cane. The bear fell dead, and to this day that old man thinks *he* killed that bear with his cane."

I sat stunned as it dawned on me what Dad had said. Mom said, "Chris, what are you talking about? What does a *bear* have to do with this? Rog just said he and Linda are going to have a baby!"

It would have been interesting to have had some sort of mind-reading devices installed on each of us at that moment to catch Mom's confusion, Linda's feeling her virtue had been questioned, and my utter glee. My feeling to this day is that Dad was joking because he was relaxing the obvious tension. He was saying, I believe in all honesty, "It's okay. We can deal with this. Let's laugh here for a moment while Rog and I share a moment of our common geezerhood."

And my polygraph reading would have said something like, "My God, there it is again. Another one of those stories that Dad tells. It's that civil ribaldry thing. He just told a slightly racy story that was okay to tell in front of the ladies because *there were no dirty words*."

In fact, there's some chance that Mom never did get what that his story is really about, a theory supported by Mom's confusion about what the heck a story about an old man and a bear had to do with what I had just told them.

Dad Instructs Me about Civil Ribaldry Even as I Thought I Was Instructing Him

For weeks I stewed on the moment Dad told the bear story. It was so superb, so glorious an example of this genre of tale and humor I had been ruminating about and, more interesting for me, a splendid illustration of the complicated circumstances leading to its telling and the remarkable style of its performance. The next time I saw Dad I asked if we could talk about something. It was never easy, not only because Dad was, as I said, deaf, but also because he was German through and through. He just didn't talk to his son. He gave orders and ruled the family, something that I later learned in his severe decline was mostly fiction. Mom, in her love for him, let him believe he ruled the roost when, in fact, as the saying goes around here, it was actually she who ruled the rooster.

My conversation with Dad on that occasion was complicated in that I had a hard time defining what it was I wanted to talk with him about, a problem that continues to this moment as I struggle to tell *you* what it is I'm talking about. As I recall I said something like this:

"Dad, you know that story you told us about the bear and the old man when Linda and I announced we were having a baby? I am trying to find out more about that kind of story. You know, without any cuss words and yet a little bit on the edgy side." I paused several times throughout this discussion to look for a sign that he might know better than I seemed to just what it was I was looking for. "You've told me a lot of those stories over the years, and I am trying to remember them and find ones I haven't heard. I'm wondering if you can help me."

Dad said nothing.

So I continued nervously, "I am thinking of a story I heard a couple weeks ago up at the Dannebrog Tavern. A guy came in all cheery and bought a round of drinks—something he wasn't known to do very often. So we asked him what was going on that made him so happy. He said that he had an old bull that wasn't doing any good in his herd, if you know what I mean. We all knew what bull he was talking about. He'd spent good money on that animal and had yet to get one good calf out of it.

"Well, he said he went to the new vet over in St. Paul and got some pills that were really supposed to be like magic. He gave that bull just two of the pills. And that bull jumped the fence, took care of all his cows, jumped another fence and took care of the neighbor's cows, and was last seen hotfooting it down the gravel road toward a dairy farmer's place about a half mile away.

"One of the other guys at the table asked, 'What do you suppose is in a pill like that that makes them so potent?'

"My friend said, 'I don't know. But they taste like peppermint.'"

Again I paused, hoping for a sign that Dad understood the kind of story I was looking for. Instead, he said, "Well, you know, Rog, that's not the end of that story." I knew enough from many decades in folklore fieldwork that it was a good time to shut up and wait for the next line. And here it came:

"One of the other guys asks, 'Did those pills do you any good?'

"And the farmer says, 'I should say they did! I made love five times today since noon!'

"Another one of his friends says, 'Well, what did your wife think about that?'

"And the farmer says, 'I don't know. I haven't been home yet.'"

I waited through another pause because I could sense Dad wasn't done with his performance yet.

"And you know, Roger," Dad continued, "that's not the end of the story either. Another one of the guys at the table says, 'Hey, I could use some pills like that. What did you do with the rest of them?'

"And the farmer says, 'I threw them down the well. And I haven't been able to get the pump handle down since.'"

Dad didn't know what to call this kind of story either, but given that he had told me precisely the kind of example I was looking for, he clearly did know what kind of stories I was talking about. His response told me that this kind of slightly prurient, incredibly subtle, rural-based form of tale truly is a genre of folktale, a distinctive narrative form that the tellers of the stories know quite well. Moreover, those who cherish and pass along such stories know what the informal, unspoken "rules" are for this form of tale: It is important, above all, that there be no obscenity. In fact, it should not include even elements that suggest obscenity, no matter what the diction. Such "jokes" must be so subtle they can be told quite comfortably in mixed company, whether that be with women (excuse the sexist nature of that parameter, but I am only describing the very real nature of this humor form and the context in which performers like Dad believe it can be told) or children.

From that moment on I made a conscious effort to collect these stories and to think about their form and nature and geography. The truth was, I didn't have to look very far. I found that this attitude—and the nature of civil ribaldry is indeed an attitude—was all around me: within my family from top to bottom; in my chosen home ground, a village in the middle of rural Nebraska; and within the historical span of my own life. Sadly I am saying with that last clause that I fear the era of the civil ribald tale is grinding to an end as its rural, traditional context fades around it. My impression is that I discovered and explored it toward the end of its tenure. I still rejoice when I hear a new story of civil ribaldry, but I feel they appear ever less often and that I may be studying a lost narrative art. That's okay. At this writing I am seventy-eight years old, so I am probably reaching the end of my vitality too. Never mind. As long as I find a new story now and then, as long as I am mentally agile enough to get the humor, and as long as I can still write them down and preserve them in the amber of the printed word, I will continue to laugh and appreciate the creativity of the folk word.

Naughty Is in the Ears of the Beholder

Piles of notes and paper, wadded-up paper bar napkins, unintelligible scribbles, and abandoned drafts and outlines for what would eventually become this book—all of it gathered dust on my office shelves. For decades I felt I could never confront the dearest people in my life with these stories or, worse yet, with some of the other more obscene, blunt, crude "jokes" I need to recount in these pages to provide a contrast that will further help delineate the boundaries of the genre of civil ribaldry. These beloved people were my gentle parents, Linda's parents, and, well, Linda herself. My beloved, blessed Linda. Our Lady of Constant Consternation. How many times have I heard her state firmly "Lady present!" as I've started a story with my buddies Mick, Dennis, John, Verne, Russ, Dave, Jim, Dick, Bondo, or . . . There are too many to list here. Turns out I'm not the only male with a junior high school–level sense of humor. In fact, I would further venture that it is the prevailing level of humor within my circle of friends.

Linda was once taking care of our dogs, big black Labradors, when Thud ("The name he earned with his head") jumped up and hit her in the mouth with his massive boulder of a head. Linda recoiled with a split lip and uttered the second-worst invective I have ever heard her say in our thirty-five years of marriage. (Brace yourself, you of tender sensitivities.) She said, and I quote, "YOU . . . YOU . . . YOU . . .

IDIOT HEAD!!!" It was a week before the dogs and I felt it was safe to come out from under the dining room table.

Oh, in case you wonder, the *worst* I have ever heard cross her lips came when we were in bed, reading on a nice, late summer evening, with the windows wide open, and a mountain lion screamed just beyond our backyard fence. Her obvious reaction was, "WHAT THE F**K WAS *THAT*?!" Even that comment fell short of the mark, considering my own reaction. Otherwise, her idea of invective runs to "gee," "darn it," and "criminy," to which I, of course, sputter, "Linda! Please! Gentleman present!"

Linda came by her genteel diction quite naturally. She tells of a time when she or one of her siblings committed some horrendous crime on mankind. When her father came home from work and learned of their sins, he blew up and sputtered, "YOU KIDS . . . YOU KIDS . . . YOU KIDS CAN JUST GO TO GRASS!" Linda still lives with the trauma of that moment and speaks of it only in hushed moments of contrition.

One of the most fascinating elements of civil ribaldry is that contradiction inherent in the apparently oxymoronic description: Is it civil? Or is it ribald? The subtlety and attractiveness of the genre is that it is both. It is a delicate balance between two common characteristics of the peasant class (and, believe me, I use that term not just with care but with affection because my family, my friends, and I myself all fall within that rubric). Honesty requires an outright recognition of the earthiness of life, but social delicacy imposes on the humor of such matters a restraint of narrative and diction. I believe it is that conflict, well meshed and buffered, that produces much of the humor of civil ribaldry. Males, who are expected to freely use the coarsest of language, demonstrate a control that in itself provides an element of humor; conversely, women, expected to be delicate flowers, surprise their audiences when they tiptoe on the perilous brink of propriety.

When Linda and I were about to be married, I made a point of introducing her to my circle of rural friends. Knowing Linda's timidity and very proper language, I was, as you can imagine, uneasy about throwing her into the mix of my considerably coarser compatriots. We were seated at the town tavern's Big Table, and precisely as I expected, my buddies started to test her, and me, by pushing the boundaries of propriety.

"Hey, Rog, this one seems a lot nicer than all those other fancy women you've hauled out here."

"I suppose you're going to trap this one down there in that log house in the woods where there's no way to get out, let alone get back to Lincoln, just like you've done with all those other poor women."

"Whatever happened to that redhead with the big tits you used to bring out here?"

"Hey, Rog, do you ever see your former wife? How about the blonde with the long legs? Are you still seeing her?"

I was genuinely worried about how Linda was dealing with this flurry of suggestive male jesting as she sat silently at the table, alone in a flood of oral testosterone. So I thought I'd relieve the pressure a bit by turning the conversation away from Linda and toward myself. Reminding my friends of our upcoming wedding date, I said, boastfully, "Yep. On April twenty-fifth there are going to be a lot of disappointed women in Nebraska."

Whereupon Linda quietly added, "Sure hope I'm not one of them."

Thus she won instant acceptance. Rather than bristling at the nature of the conversation, she joined it. Just that fast she had defused any questions about her sense of humor . . . and yet, just as important, she had done it in her own way . . .

quietly and with language well within the bounds of decency. She showed my friends, and not just incidentally *me*, that while the language may be subtle, she was not far removed from her own peasant roots.

Similarly when I was once joking with her in company about being a Catholic Bohemian, she turned the comments outward, remarkably, by turning them inward: "The only problem with being a Catholic Bohemian girl is that as a Catholic you only have six safe days a month. But being a Bohemian, you forget which days they are."

Thus, this "delicate flower" showed that she is quite aware of her sexuality, her ethnicity, and by violating the boundaries only slightly, the expectations of propriety. The exact opposite occurs when expectations of coarseness are met with demonstrations of propriety. Who's tougher than cowboys? Nobody. So we expect the roughest diction from them. And it's not just a matter of the cowboys imposing decent diction on others, as in the story about my father and the cowboys at the JayEm Ranch, but also in demonstrating their own constraints.

I once got into some minor trouble when I was writing essays for my "Postcards from Nebraska" for CBS News' *CBS Sunday Morning* with Charles Kuralt (1987–2001). In expressing my annual dismay when a late frost inevitably froze and killed the flowers on my beloved lilac bush, I used the word "damn" three times. As in "it happens every damn year." Kuralt got lots of mail from people unhappy with that word popping up during their Sunday morning breakfast, but he said on air that "damn it, that was the best word for the unhappy circumstances."

All the fuss was worth one letter I received from (who else?!) a Wyoming cowboy who said that the phrase "every damn time" was in fact insufficient for disasters like freeze-burned lilacs, and if I didn't step my cursing up a notch the next time I talked about such natural disasters, he would "come to Dannebrog and wash my mouth out with whiskey."

Early in my research into folklore of the West, I encountered frequent mentions of "bear sign," which the context told me was a cherished good stuff. As a cowboy explained to me, the term refers to pan-fried doughnuts, which . . . if you squint a bit, I suppose . . . look a little like bear "sign." Which is to say, bear poop. We also find this sort of euphemism in old cowboy ballads like "Whoopee Ti Yi Yo!," where the cowboy's occupation is summarized as "early in the springtime we round up them doggies / mark 'em, brand 'em, bob off their tails."

"Bob off their tails?" I found no references to a custom of cutting tails off of calves. Yes, sometimes cattle are dehorned. That is clear enough. But removing their tails? And, of course, the male calves are made steers by . . . Uh-oh. I get it. "Bobbing off" their, uh, "tails." Wouldn't want to say "castrate" in polite company.

While working with the folk language appendix to a book I co-edited titled *Wyoming Folklore: Reminiscences, Folktales, Beliefs, Customs, and Folk Speech,* I was particularly amused by the term "roughlock" as used by loggers. Its main definition in the Federal Writers' Project materials was "a chain that is fastened under and around the runners of the heavy sleds used in hauling logs and railroad ties; the chains cut into the ice and snow of the road and prevent the sleds from gaining too much momentum down the hills." But its alternate definition was what caught my attention and tickled my sense of humor: "also cheese and cheese products." A lesson in how to be coarse without being, well, coarse.

A First Lesson in Military Nomenclature

And then there's my sainted (no exaggeration) mother. She once read one of my books, and when I asked her how she liked it, she put down her sewing, looked at me seriously, and said to my chagrin, "Roger, it's a nice book, but I think you know how I feel about anyone using the 'F-word.'" My mind raced as I tried to imagine where that word might have slipped into my book. I don't recall ever having used that word in print. Ever. I suspect that that comes in part from the deep trauma I experienced sixty years ago when I came home from my first year of summer encampment with the Nebraska Air National Guard. In the good old days, all young men had a seven-year military obligation, which was fine with me, and when I was still sixteen, I joined the guard. My first monthly meeting was with a unit having its first meeting on home ground after returning from a stint in the Korean War. So this apple-cheeked lad was tossed in with the unit's grizzled combat veterans, and my education began at once.

Uh-oh. Here I go, off on a tangent. But it's relevant to the explorations of this book, so I will ask your patience and promise to return to the topic at hand as quickly as I can.

At one of my first meetings with the Nebraska Air National Guard, in my shiny new uniform, one of the rumpled vets handed me some papers and said, "Airman Welsch, check out a vehicle from the motor pool and go to whatever radio supply outlets you can find in town and get us this part,

ASAP." Good grief, I had only had a driver's license for a year, and here I was, being sent out on a military mission! He handed me an official U.S. Air Force requisition form for the part I was to locate and bring back to my unit. I was in a communications unit so it made all the sense in the world to me that we needed electronic parts, but it was still flattering that I was being entrusted with the mission.

In uniform and with a military pickup truck, I went from one electronic supply source to another around Lincoln, Nebraska, looking for the needed part. I would hand the requisition form to the man at the front desk, and he would look it over, look at me (presumably to verify my official status), and tell me to check with the women back in the office for the component indicated on the official U.S. Air Force requisition form. And I did. Each cheerfully told me she couldn't help me, but then she provided me with yet another possible source for the part. I duly went with my official U.S. Air Force requisition form to every spot and encountered the same frustration. As helpful as everyone was, including the secretaries and stock ladies in the shops, no one was able to provide me with the needed part.

When the weekend was over, my father asked me how my first military experience had gone, and I proudly told him about the trust that Sergeant Schwabauer had put in me and the frustration I felt in not having fulfilled the assigned mission. "Let me see that official United States Air Force requisition form," he said. I handed it to him. He read it, rolled his eyes, and handed it back to me. I don't recall what he said, but it was enough to bring clarity to the situation: I had spent two full days going to Lincoln electronics supply outlets in search of, the official U.S. Air Force requisition form said, a "fallopian tube."

Fortunately I was a fast learner. Recently Sergeant Schwabauer, who eventually became a friend, wrote me shortly before his death and said, to my pride and his admiration, that I was the worst soldier he had ever encountered in his long military career. For him I was a problem; for the commanding officer of our unit I became a resource he could count on for any un-military . . . no, non-military . . . sometimes ANTI-military assignment he needed done confidentially. I made Ernie Bilko look like a piker. I may have been the worst soldier Sergeant Schwabauer ever encountered, but he knew as well as I did that I was the best secret agent that unit ever had. I can probably boast that now and then I even accomplished the impossible.

In fact, I was too good. Seventeen and just home from two weeks in the tutelage of this band of thieves, rogues, rascals, and give-a-shits, I was ready to conquer the world. Until I returned home from that first summer encampment and sat down for my first meal at the family table with Mom and Dad. I was tanned and fit, immortal and arrogant . . . until the moment when, without so much as realizing the moment, I said, "Dad, please pass the f**king potatoes."

No one said a word. No one needed to. Sergeant Schwabauer could have profited from learning the power of that silence from my father and mother. It would have saved him a lot of yelling and swearing over the next seven years. That silence hung in the air like the aura of a sour diaper bucket. It was withering, searing, nuclear.

All of which is to say, I did not inherit my parents' gentility. However (to get back to the story I started about my mother and her disapproval of my using the "F-word" in my book), I do use appropriate caution and consider my audience when shifting vernacular gears. So I was genuinely baffled by her dismay because I could not think of any circumstance in which I might have used that word in my writing. As I sat baffled, Mom continued with her chastisement, and I gradually sorted out what the problem was. In my book about old age, *Golden Years My Ass: Adventures in Geriatric Indignities*, I had indeed used an F-word. But not the F-word that is usually thought of as being *the* F-word. I had referred in that book to myself as—brace yourself—an "old fart."

Since that moment I have had warm thoughts of my sainted mother hearing references on television (certainly not in the social circles she was in!) to . . . "the F-word." And she thought they were speaking of that other forbidden F-word—"fart." That's how dear my mother was.

Diction Friction

It's one thing to say I never heard my father curse but quite another to say the same about my mother. I don't think I ever heard her say so much as "dang." A legend in our family tells of a time when she was driving somewhere with my two daughters, Jenny and Joyce, when they were very young. Apparently they were making girlie noises in the backseat of Mom's car and were distracting her, so she asked what was going on back there. Joyce, being her father's daughter, said, "Jenny farted."

Mom, being my mother, said, "Joyce! Ladies do not 'fart.'"

Joyce asked, "Well, what do girls do?"

Mom replied, "Girls *fluff*."

Which means my girls grew up giggling at every television commercial promising "fluffy rice."

Buddy Hackett once noted that women do not fart. But, he added, they sometimes stand near dogs that do.

My father insisted that women do not "sweat." He explained, "Horses sweat. Men perspire. And women . . . glow."

Even Dad's "civil ribaldries" scandalized my mother but not so much that he was forbidden to tell them. She would simply roll her eyes and sputter in two long, distinct syllables, "Chriiii-uuus." In his declining years Dad spent a lot of time in doctors' offices and hospitals, with Mom, of course, in attendance. In his final hours he did himself and me proud: he told Mom he loved her, he flirted with a nurse, and he made us laugh. On one earlier and notable medical occasion, he was attended to by a truly gorgeous female doctor. He was in rough condition, but even then he managed to rise to the occasion. The Hollywood-worthy doctor applied pressure with her fingers on his shoulders and asked if it hurt. Dad said it did not. Then his chest. No pain. Then his abdomen. No. His groin . . .

Uh-oh. I could see where this one was going. After a pause, Dad said, "Actually, you know . . . that's starting to feel pretty good."

And Mom said, "Chriiii-uuus!" In two syllables.

One of Dad's favorite stories, always when my mother was within earshot, was about the time they went to the doctor for their annual checkups. Dad passed his examination with flying colors, but then the doctor asked him if he had any questions or if he had any problems or symptoms he wanted to ask about. As Dad told the story, he then told the doctor that, yes, there was one thing that gave him some concern, so of course the doctor asked him to describe the problem. Dad said, "Well, doctor, I am worried because I sweat so bad the second time my wife, Bertha, and I make love." The doctor said he'd look into the problem and try to have an answer for Dad later.

Then the doctor checked out Mom and declared that she was in pretty good condition, considering her age. But he added that he was concerned about Dad's report of his sweating so badly the second time he made love to her.

"Well, the old fool!" Mom said. "The second time we make love is usually in August!"

Whereupon every time Dad told this story, Mom would say from wherever she happened to be during Dad's performance, "Chriiii-uuus!" In two syllables.

Evoked and Provoked

I hadn't come up with the phrase "civil ribaldry," nor formulated a clear idea of what I was trying to describe by it, when I bought a small parcel of agricultural land along the Middle Loup River in central Nebraska in 1974. In fact, I bought the ground without so much as driving to the little village of Dannebrog just over the hill from the site. But as I came to know the town, the countryside around it, and the cast of characters who were my new neighbors, I realized that I had somehow stumbled onto a gold mine of resources for my longtime interest in folk humor. By that time I had published two books about folk humor, mostly about the tall tale—*Shingling the Fog and Other Plains Lies* and *Catfish at the Pump*—and they're both still in print with the University of Nebraska Press. In Dannebrog and surrounding Howard County not only did I continue to find the tall tale alive and well (although maybe just a little on the puny side) but I also found that I was hearing more and more stories similar to those I had always admired from my father's telling. It seemed that my father and mother were not the only people who appreciated a gentility of diction and narrative while nonetheless embracing a mildly bawdy sense of humor.

Bumps Nielsen was the rural mail carrier in Dannebrog, and I quickly learned that Bumps was a central character in all things Dannebrognabian. He came with a complete cast of characters in the form of his own family: his wife,

Harriett, who is still an institution here; his son, Eric, who fully inherited his father's sense of humor and knack for telling stories; and his daughter, Ramona, of equal wit. One of the first stories I recall hearing from Bumps was about the time his uncle Jim was standing in the village's main street, talking with a friend, when the friend heard a totally new sound and looked up to see . . . the first airplane that had ever flown over the area. Imagine what an event that must have been! Forever nothing had appeared in that azure but birds, clouds, and maybe now and then a tumbleweed or bumblebee, and now, here above them, was a man. In a machine! I can imagine it must have been quite a moment. The startled friend, with both feet firmly planted on the ground sputtered, "Why, Jim, look at that! It's one of them mail planes!"

Uncle Jim drawled laconically, "Nah. Them's just the wheels hangin' down."

It was not long before I made a point of appearing at the Chew 'n' Chat Café in the mornings and the village tavern in the evenings, as much for the entertainment as for the refreshments. And when there was an empty chair at "the Big Table" near Bumps, that was my destination. My appreciation was apparently obvious. Before long whenever someone told a particularly good story, someone else would hand me a paper napkin, because they had grown accustomed to my habit of scribbling a few quick notes so I wouldn't forget the stories all while I struggled to keep from choking on my laughter.

One of the characteristics of civil ribaldry, as with a good deal of folklore, is that it is unself-consciously evoked by context. What that fancy talk means is that you can't ask someone to tell you such stories because that's not the way people store them in their minds. It takes some kind of trigger in the events or conversations of the moment to open the mental doors that let that particular story come forth.

It's not as if someone at the Big Table said, "Okay, everyone, pay attention. Now we're going to tell those stories Rog likes and refers to as 'civil ribaldry.' Bumps, you start . . ." That's not the way it works.

My father was a treasury not just of the kind of stories I am dealing with here but also of German proverbs. He had a proverb for every circumstance. And that's the point: it took a circumstance to evoke the appropriate proverb. *Eigenlob schtinkt!* (Self-praise stinks!) *Armudje! Armudje!* (Oh, the squalor!) *Wer nicht hört, muss fühl!* (He who doesn't listen has to suffer!) *Die Augen sind grösser als der Magen.* (Your eyes are bigger than your stomach.) Perhaps you have sensed that it was usually my presence or behavior that triggered these traditional responses from my father's inventory!

At some point I thought I should collect Dad's pungent and traditional German wisdom, if for no other reason than for the family archives. So I told Dad what I wanted to do, fed him a couple examples of what I was looking for, and sat back with my pen and paper to record the flood of proverbs I knew he had in his inventory. We sat there. Nothing. Of course, there was nothing. That's not the way proverbs work. There had to be some event or comment or person (me!) who needed sound wisdom, and that, in turn, would trigger Dad to call forth the nuggets. I couldn't simply ask for them and expect them to pop into Dad's cerebral cortex. I needed to be there when circumstances invited the fitting proverb.

And so it is with civil ribaldry. I couldn't ask Bumps or anyone else to provide me with such narratives, even if I tried to prime that pump with some stories I had previously heard. I had to wait patiently and listen closely. Sometimes the conversations at the café or tavern were about foibles and exploits of our rural fire department. Since these stories too are interesting and more often than not funny, I sat and listened and laughed. For no reason at all other than the flow of the conversation, the topic might be, oh, memorable fistfights in the town. Or barn dances. Or Uncle Jim. Or . . . whatever. And then, suddenly, to my surprise and delight, there it would be . . . another story that I considered "civil ribaldry" and had hoped to find.

Scene: Big Table in Dannebrog's Chew 'n' Chat Café. *Time*: Some day, any day. *Action*: The conversation was of the news of the day, and quite casually someone mentioned that a young lady in town who, er, was particularly popular with the young fellows—with quite a few young fellows, if you know what I mean—had turned up pregnant. Again. Someone at the table asked rhetorically, "Who do you suppose the father of that baby is?"

And Bumps said, "That's like trying to guess which tooth on a buzz saw hits the board first."

It's not exactly a *story*, more like folk poetry, I suppose, but it is a turn of phrase that has stuck with me these thirty-some years later. I have never heard anyone else say that. Ever. So if I hadn't been there at that moment on that day, I probably would never have heard that splendid gem of rural simile. I had to be there. As I was on the morning that Bumps came in a bit later than usual and looking a trifle more haggard than usual, even though no one would ever have described him as dapper. Someone at the Big Table asked him where he'd been and what was going on.

"I was just over to Doc Jones for a proctologic exam."

"What's a prolit . . . practilog . . . procti . . . that thing you just said, Bumps?"

"A proctologic exam. What it is, is Doc Jones has you drop your britches and bend over his examination table. Then he puts his right hand on your right shoulder, and his left hand on your left shoulder, and . . ." After a long, dramatic pause, he exclaimed, "Why, that son of a bitch!"

Okay, Bumps's language may not have been all that civil, but as with Linda's exclamation when we heard the mountain lion in the bottom ground or mine when a late frost once again destroys the lilacs, the language has to fit the situation.

I can't help but wonder how many stories like this one were told around some table during the century before I came to Dannebrog but never came up afterward. Or how many were told at the café, the tavern, or the Co-op when I was in Lincoln and not in Dannebrog. Or popped up in the hours before I came to town for the mail or after I had picked up the mail and gone back home. Or how many were told in the café while I was in the tavern or in the tavern when I was in Kerry's Grocery. How many are being told up at the Legion Club at this very moment while I sit here writing these words?

The inescapable conclusion has to be that whatever examples I have collected over the decades, however many I have remembered, whatever scribbles on bar napkins survived Linda's washing machine, and whatever wasn't subsequently lost here in one of the piles on my desk can only represent a sliver of this grand tradition of folk humor. So many stories, so little time.

Cipherin'

Another common characteristic of this genre of humor is that its specificity hints of the modern legend. The traditional, age-old legend was a way of explaining the inexplicable. In a world full of questions and bewildering things before and through the Middle Ages, the legend explained things: why certain mountains were considered sacred or had names like "King's Mound"; why natural events such as eclipses, comets, disease, caves, plagues, or floods happened; why things as mundane as curious names for plants developed. In a world of mystery, the legend provided an explanation. But the modern legend is exactly the opposite. It hasn't helped that the modern legend has been cursed with a misleading label, "urban legend," because it is not urban. It is modern. It is indeed a new legend form, but this time it has arisen to provide mystery in a world where there are too many answers and not nearly enough surprises. You may or may not recall any of the ancient legends or you may have only read about them in books; they are not very current these days. But I know for certain that you have encountered the *modern* legend. They usually follow a framework: "A friend of my cousin Dorothy knows this guy who was vacationing in Thailand and woke up in a hotel bathtub full of ice one morning to find . . . *one of his kidneys had been removed*!" They always have enough details to lend specificity and therefore authenticity to the story, which inevitably also contains an element of surprise and mystery.

The stories of civil ribaldry have some of those aspects. In fact, I have to be careful in telling some of the stories to you, because I don't want to hurt anyone's feelings where specific names were used in the stories I originally heard. Are they truly anecdotes from personal experience? Or are they stories that, as with folk jokes, have passed from person to person, being polished along the way until they are like naturally burnished gems in a riverbed? Hard to say. Moreover, I'm not sure it's important. It's not exactly lying . . . It's performance.

Was Bumps Nielsen really abused by Doc Jones under the guise of a proctologic exam? Of course not. Had he just come from Jones's office? Where he had a proctologic examination? Maybe. Probably. Or was his visit to the doctor's office merely the event that triggered Bumps's recall of a story that he'd heard somewhere else, perhaps long ago?

I think of a time I went into the Dannebrog Tavern and spotted an old friend, a horse trader, sitting at the bar and looking a bit glum. I sat down beside him, bought him a drink, and asked him what was going on in his life. He said that he had just been involved in a trade that had left him somewhat confused. I urged him to tell me the story.

He said that a man had just been to his place, looking at a mare he had for sale. The guy said he'd buy the horse, but he wanted a 15 percent discount for paying cash in the exchange. My friend said he had "ciphered" endlessly trying to figure out what 15 percent of $175 would be, and his answers had never come out the same twice.

He explained, "So I went over to Ms. [name omitted for decency and legal reasons]—you know, the schoolmarm—because I figured she'd know how to calkalate [his pronunciation] the sum. I knocked at her door, and she opened it up for me so I posed the problem: 'How much would you take off if I offered you a hundred seventy-five dollars for something but wanted a fifteen percent discount for paying cash?'

"And she says to me, 'Everything but my socks and earrings.'"

My friend returned to his whiskey, shaking his head in bewilderment. And I was left to laugh and wonder, if only a little bit, if I had just heard a bit of personal oral history, a rumor, or a joke. To my mind, however, a definitive classification is not important. For me, as a folklorist, I had just been a participant, if only as an audience of one, in a superbly performed piece of one-act folk theater.

I probably should have applauded and shouted, "Bravo!" And then I should've asked for an encore.

Thinking Fast

Do stories of civil ribaldry come from actual experiences? That is, did these things actually happen? Or are they perhaps the product of particularly inventive minds? Folklorists have wrestled for generations with the problem of where folklore comes from. Are some ideas so universally human that they arise independently at many points in history and geography? Or do they spring from one place and then over time find wide geographic distribution? It truly is a mystery and not one I think is likely to be figured out soon. In fact, more than likely, both theories may be true. What matters to the practical folklorist is that however they are generated, materials like these stories find an appreciative audience and enter the "folk mouth." That is, someone hears the story, likes it, and passes it along to others, perhaps with some minor improvements. There is an old saying among tall-tale tellers that one is permitted to improve any story by 10 percent at each telling.

Whatever the origin(s), a story finds some currency and spreads. Some people are not good storytellers and make the story less interesting or attractive. Although I have no way of knowing how such an arcane process can ever be investigated or, for that matter, discovered, I imagine a poorly told version doesn't go much further. But a story that takes on even the slightest improvement is likely to find an even wider and more appreciative audience. When it comes to how such stories develop and are as well crafted as they are,

I am an advocate of evolution, not intelligent design. There are raconteurs—a word that was once defined for me as "a fancy word for a particularly gifted bullshitter"—who are indeed gifted storytellers and are the most likely people to have a general gift for clever turns of phrase and narrative; but the touchstone of the folktale specifically and of folklore in general is the polish that comes from repeated transmission, from one gifted storyteller to another and to another. In my sixty years of working with folklore and especially folk humor, I have yet to encounter anyone who is a story inventor. Storytellers—but not originators.

Annually I pitch a fit when some teacher(s) writes to me or talks to me about a class assignment he or she is working on that requires the children to write tall tales. I respond that I have every intention of reporting them to Social Services for abusing the tykes in their class. I have never met an adult who can compose a tall tale worth the telling. It just isn't done. Somewhere an exaggeration arises, and over time and space and telling and retelling by many, perhaps by generations of master storytellers, it becomes the polished gem that captures the attention of even the erudite professor at the tavern table.

No, I take that back. I have met some people who are capable of creating a tall tale. In fact, maybe Bumps Nielsen invented that line about the buzz saw hitting the board. But it surely isn't child's play. Just a few days ago as I write this, I was with my old buddy Mick, having chicken fried steaks at the town tavern, when in walked Jerry Fanta. I introduced the two men, and they shook hands, with Jerry's massive mitt engulfing Mick's hand as if it were a potato chip. Mick is a brick mason and a Marine, so it's not as if he's a pansy, but Jerry's hands are truly objects of awe. As Jerry walked off, I commented to Mick that Jerry plays the accordion. Mick said, "I bet he can play it with one hand." Now that is a genius bit of wit, something Mick can do. And I can't. I'm not that quick. Mick is. Linda is. My friend Eric is. But not me. Not more than a half dozen of the thousands of people I have come to know in my long life are that quick. But certainly never a child. Those teachers might just as well be asking their pupils to write a Shakespearean drama or to paint a Rembrandt.

Elsewhere I mentioned the Nielsen family of my little village of Dannebrog: Harriett, Bumps, and their children, Eric and Ramona. All are friends of mine and gifted storytellers with finely honed senses of humor. Even when he seems to be making casual conversation, Eric's diction is that of the master storyteller. Even when the conversation is in completely ordinary contexts. Or, for that matter, quite out-of-the-ordinary contexts. Once he and I were floating down a mile or two of the river that abuts my acreage, gathering up orphaned fence and telephone posts that had been uprooted by a recent flood. We were roping together a sizable raft of poles and posts and floating along with them on a leisurely, warm June day, chatting and watching the banks and sandbars for more treasures, when somehow our conversation turned to the fact that I was considering getting a vasectomy. I was scouting around my male friends to get their feelings and experiences about the procedure.

After a pause, Eric said somewhat sheepishly that he had not only considered getting a vasectomy and had gone through "the most painful part" of the procedure but had also backed out before the final snips, so to speak.

As you can imagine, that was a provocative comment, so of course I asked him what had happened. He said, "Rog, I was all set for the operation. I went to the doctor's office, got into the hospital gown, was laid out on the table. They got me all prepped, and then . . . they rolled in a tray of knives, scissors, clamps, and other weird shiny things I can't imagine uses for. I took one look at all that and said, 'No, thanks,' and that was the end of it."

"But . . . but what was the most painful part of *that*?" I asked.

"Rog, when they tore off the tape they'd used to hold my wiener up out of the way, it tore all the hair off my chest."

I am not joking when I say that the delivery of that story almost killed me, because I lost my hold on our log raft. I went down in the river three times before I could regain control of myself and grab a hold again of our raft.

I remember a time when Eric commented on my pronounced duck walk, with my toes pointing out almost at ninety degrees from the line of my path. He said, "Looking at your footprints in the snow, I can't tell which way you're going." There are so many ways he could have joked about my gait, but his talent lies with having that ear for folk poetry, a gift he probably got from his father, Bumps.

I also think of a time when that quick wit Mick was flirting with a barmaid, and I joked, "Be careful, Mick. You're a married man after all."

And he said, "Yeah, but I'm not fanatical about it."

While my interest runs more toward the traditional inventory of stories that are in the general repertoire of the broader community, there seems also to be an element of individual wit inherent in the role of the teller. Those of us who call ourselves folklorists are always on the lookout for what we call "carriers" or "tradition keepers." It seems that there is often a person in any group or community who has become something of a specialist, something of a folklorist himself or herself, and who almost unself-consciously pays attention to such things as stories, anecdotes, tales, jokes, smart remarks, anything interesting, and has a talent for recalling and retelling them. That person is likely to be the best one to sit next to in the tavern when a crowd starts telling stories and asks about the time the priest walked in on Lumir on a Friday just as he sat down to a plate of sausage. Or what *was* that story about the fight that started in front of the bar and worked its way all down the main street to the cemetery? Or *was* that famous dance hall in Dannebrog called Pleasure Isle? That person will be the best resource not just for the kind of story the collector is interested in but also for a rich treasury of proverbs, jokes, recipes, straight history, dates and names, even traditional songs and music. It doesn't hurt if that person is somehow central to community activities . . . a renowned cook like Harriett Nelson, a rural mail carrier like her late husband, Bumps, or the town tavern owner like their son, Eric. It is also from members of a dynasty like the Nielsens or from wits such as my wife Linda that one is most likely to hear not just traditional materials but also individually created, idiosyncratic humor. Logically enough, just as they are enthusiastic conveyers of *traditional* materials and just as they have the best ear and memory for the wit of others, they also have the talent for creating memorable lines of their own, high points of lively conversations, and sometimes downright poetry, which those present often remember and repeat time and time again for many years. That is, what starts as individual invention becomes folklore.

There is not a doubt in my mind or in Linda's that at the heart of our own enduring love is her brilliant wit. She claims, and I believe her, that she often doesn't know from where her bon mots come. Without any apparent thought on her part, the comments are suddenly there in just the right diction and with perfect timing. A young woman once commented disapprovingly to Linda about the naughty girl calendars hanging in my tractor repair shop and asked her why she put up with such disgusting misbehavior. Linda replied with a line so perfect I have never forgotten its brilliance: "Beth, sometimes it's easier just to keep an old engine idling than to jump-start it fresh every time."

I was watching a Sunday morning political discussion

show once and commented to no one in particular but within Linda's hearing, "I wonder if Condoleezza Rice ever wonders how she got hooked up with that ignorant boob?"

Linda commented, also to no one in particular but within *my* hearing, "Sooner or later, every woman asks herself that question."

Similarly while watching a news report about a woman in a nearby town who had tried to hire a gunman to shoot her husband but the would-be assassin turned out (as they almost always do) to be an undercover cop, I asked, "Linda, would you ever try to hire someone to shoot me?"

"No," she said. "I'd just go up to town and ask for volunteers."

I envy Linda's ready wit, timing, and comic diction even though I am often as not her victim. Linda and I have talked about her talent. She freely admits that not only does she have no idea where it comes from but also she doesn't know when it will explode onto the scene or what she will say. In fact, she sometimes worries that one of these days she will say something without thinking—which is the way it works—and find that she has gotten herself, or the both of us, into real trouble.

We were once having a conversation about my upcoming birthday, and she asked me what I would like for my special day. Thinking I was making a clever joke, I said, "You know, how about that three-way I've always wanted?"

"Fine," she said, "I think that's a great idea."

I waited for the punch line, but with her comedic skill, she was silent while I puzzled why she would so easily agree to a sexual triangle for her geezerly husband. Then she added, "But I won't be one of the women in bed naked with you."

Now I was really puzzled. My sweet, gentle wife, as faithful and proper a woman as you can know, was agreeing not only to my having sex with two women at once but now . . . she was not going to be one of them? Uuuuuh . . . again

I was completely baffled as to where she was headed with this conversation.

Without my asking, she explained her reasoning: "Rog, I mean, after all, what are the odds of you getting a strange woman into bed with you naked? Maybe—what?—one in a million? But *two* strange women naked in bed with you? Dear, they just don't make odds that big."

Thus endeth the conversation.

My friend Eric often exhibits the same kind of spontaneous creativity, a talent that escapes me. We once met on the main street of Dannebrog, and he asked me how I was doing. I replied that I wasn't doing all that well because I'd just been diagnosed with prostate cancer. Eric paused only a moment before expressing his concern: "Wow. Rog, there are going to be a lot of unhappy people here in town when they hear that." After a perfectly timed dramatic pause, he continued, "Most of the money in the pool at the tavern is on your liver."

It is my impression after fifty years of working in the field of folklore that a lot of the rural wit I find most interesting is not a matter of memory or conscious invention but a manner of thinking, a talent for timing, a flair for diction and detail. I was once involved in a conversation with some local farming friends of mine when one told us breathlessly that two strangers—obviously city boys—had approached him that morning about the possibility of his allowing them to plant a quarter-acre plot of marijuana in the middle of one of his irrigated cornfields. "Why, those fellows told me that I could make enough money on a patch that big to pay my rent on the whole field for two months," my friend exulted.

"Hell, that's nothing," said Neil, another rural friend. Putting his forefingers and thumbs together to form a triangle, he explained, "There are ladies in Omaha who make enough money in a couple nights with a patch just *this* big to pay the rent on fancy city apartments all *year*!"

I'm sure these conversational bon mots were indeed coinages of particularly creative minds. While I remembered them and have told them as personal anecdotes in many contexts, as well as now in these pages, I have not seen that they have entered into wider circulation—which is to say, to have become folklore. I wonder if those who uttered the clever comments remember them. But to my mind they speak nonetheless to the kind of mind-set that nurtures civil ribaldry. It's no accident that the people who are most creative in their own conversations are the very ones who appreciate, remember, and convey the kinds of stories I call civil ribaldry and present here. Within schools of folklore scholarship some discuss the "folk mind," the kind of personality that values and therefore preserves and disseminates folklore—that is, legend, proverb, foodways, the full gamut of the traditional. Within Native American circles these folks are often referred to as "tradition keepers." As with any authentic folk artist, these human storehouses are not likely to think of themselves that way and certainly never refer to themselves as such. For those of us who enjoy folk humor casually and conversationally or who find it fertile ground for understanding tradition, though, there *is* a folk mind; and finding one, or a community inclined to a traditional form such as civil ribaldry, is similar to finding a mountain stream glittering with flakes of gold.

Cold . . . and Deep

The element that triggers the recall and recitation of a tale of civil ribaldry may be something quite outside the immediate context of the telling . . . maybe a visit to a doctor's office or a horse trade miles and hours away from the opportunity to spin the yarn. Even when more immediate, a segue from normal conversation to the recitation of the tale may go almost undetected. Someone at the Big Table wonders where my friend Kenny has been since he hasn't been at the table for some time. Eric suggests that he may have been out working in the fields, adding, "I was driving the gravel to St. Paul a couple days ago and saw Kenny out on a tractor pulling a harrow. I was kind of curious because I noticed as he turned at the road end of the furrow that he was sitting on that tractor stark naked from the waist down."

Others at the table shared expressions of wonderment. Eric said, "Yeah, I'd say so! I waited until he came back across the field and waved him down. I asked, 'What was that all about, no pants . . . half naked like that?'

"Kenny said, 'I worked out here all day yesterday without a shirt on and came home with a stiff neck. This,' he said while pointing down to his absent pants, 'was my wife's idea.'"

Such stories gain all the more credibility at the Big Table by being embedded in conversations in which genuinely true stories are narrated. And stories no less remarkable. For example, someone—maybe even Lyle himself—along the way reported that Lyle Fries had complained the week before about the barrel under his outhouse being filled to the brim. Someone had logically asked if he had poked holes in the bottom before he installed it under the privy. Lyle had said no, he hadn't thought of doing that at the time. So when some smart aleck suggested that it wasn't too late and that Lyle should take his .30-30 rifle and shoot down through the outhouse seat to make the appropriate punctures in the barrel below, everyone at that table could easily imagine the consequences of blasting down into the barrel with a high-powered rifle. Then Lyle, an honest man with a superior sense of humor, returned the next day to report on the consequences himself.

That tale elicited yet again the story about the time, again not long ago, when Mel and Gary were fishing over at the state lake. Mel went into the provided park privy, lowered the bib of his overalls, and saw his checkbook drop down into the mire and morass below. Now a sensible man would have just poked that checkbook down under the surface since he surely wasn't going to be able to use it ever again and could have easily replaced it when he got back to town. But no, Mel insisted that he wanted to retrieve the checkbook, ostensibly to avoid identity theft—as if anyone else would even see, let alone try to fish out, that sodden paper. Mel poked around with a stick but had no luck, so Gary, ever a source of good ideas, suggested that what they needed to do was get a better view of the problem. They wadded up a bunch of toilet paper on the end of the stick, lit it on fire, and put it down the toilet seat's hole. When it reached the level of the methane pool below, it ignited an explosion that pretty much destroyed the outhouse. Gary and Mel fled the scene, fearing prosecution for destroying government property. Another contributor to the conversation suggested that the best solution would have been for Gary, a large fellow, simply to grab Mel, the more diminutive of the pair, by the ankles and lower him down into the privy to retrieve the lost checkbook.

The scene at that Big Table had been set for further storytelling. The context was established for outhouse stories. And explosions. And thus we heard the venerable tale, well established and widely told and published, about the gent who goes to the outhouse, which was recently "freshened" with a liberal sprinkling of kerosene. The old-timer knocks the dodder out of his still-lit pipe into the hole beside the one he is seated on. The resulting explosion threw him twenty yards into the farmyard, and there he sat up and said (choose one): (1) "Must have been something I et," or (2) "Good thing I didn't let that one go in the house."

In-house Outhouses

On the occasion of telling an outhouse anecdote, story, joke, or legend, it triggered another, and that particular conversation at the café's breakfast table went on almost to the noon hour. A widely known and appreciated story, usually told in an exaggerated Danish accents tells of three old immigrants who got to arguing once in the town tavern about which of them could dig the best outhouse base. The first puts forth his skills, saying, "I takes my shofel, and I digs and digs, and den I puts de outhouse over dat hole. Ven I take down my overhauls and poops, I count, 'Vun, two, tree, four.' Den I hears 'plop,' and she hits de bottom of dat hole."

The second old Dane snorts indignantly and says, "Vel den, Lars, ven I digs a hole for my privy, I takes my shofel, and I digs and digs and digs and den digs some more. I puts de outhouse over dat hole. Ven I take down my overhauls and poops, I count, 'Vun, two, tree, four, twenty, tirty.' Den I hears 'plop,' and she hits de bottom of dat hole."

Finally Nels gets his turn and he says, "Ven I digs a hole for my privy, I takes my shofel, and I digs and digs and digs and digs and digs and digs, den digs some more. I puts de outhouse over dat hole. Ven I take down my overhauls and poops, I count, 'Vun, two, tree, four, twenty, tirty, ninety, a hundert.' Den I gets up and looks down behind me, and ders dat poop, hanging in my overhaul straps just like always."

Whatever discomfort outhouses have provided mankind

over the centuries is nothing, it would seem, compared to the amount of material they have provided for humor. An old-time Czech farmer is found fishing around in his outhouse with a stick and is asked what happened. He says he dropped his shirt down the hole when he was taking off his overall straps. The onlooker is amazed that he would go through that much trouble for an old shirt that is filthy beyond possible use now. The old-timer explains, "Oh no, I vouldn't go tru dis trouble for dat shirt, oh no. But der vas a kolache in de pocket!" (For anyone who doesn't live in Nebraska or the Czech Republic, the pastry called *kolache*—KO-lawtch or ko-LAWTCH-ee—is what the *runza* is to the German Russian or the pierogi is to the Ukrainian.)

Old privy sites are particularly fruitful discoveries for archeologists because everything from money to pistols fell through the hole as the visitors prepared to be seated. It was also a place where empty whiskey, bitters, or lady's tonic bottles could be disposed of without any danger of discovery by the disapproving. Again an old farmer is seen throwing a twenty-dollar bill down the hole of his privy and is asked why he is doing such a crazy thing. He explains that he dropped a dollar bill down the hole when he first came in and asks, "Do you really think I'm going to go through all this muck for nothing more than a dollar bill?"

Or what about the couple whose child fell into the hole under the outhouse? When they were asked why they didn't fish him out, they explained they figured it would be easier to make a new one than fish out and clean up the other one.

The outhouse was a veritable font of rural humor. (If your humor runs to the scatological, see my book *Outhouses*). The structure of the "private place," as a proper rural gent once described it to me, was generally and logically reserved for acts of defecation and urination. But as with sex, we humans seem to find our most basic biological functions to be a source of amusement and laughter. A rare combination of the tall tale and civil ribaldry is found in the story that is told in my own Danish-founded village of Dannebrog. Two old settlers are returning from an evening at the town tavern and cross the bridge over the Middle Loup River, which sits just below where I write these words. When they stop on the bridge to relieve themselves over the railing, one of them makes an offhanded boast, "That water sure is cold!" The other responds, "And deep!"

Some of these tales appear in conversations only now and then, with the circumstances that evoke them being rare themselves; others are as recurrent as the very function in which their humor lies. It doesn't matter how often they might be told, when the opening lines are recognized as an introduction to an old favorite, everyone laughs, if for no other reason than because everyone else is laughing. That's always a good idea. You surely don't want to let anyone think you're too dumb to get the joke, after all.

Then someone clears his throat and says, "That reminds me of the time old Lars Jensen over by Nysted, just north of the school, got tired of listening to Esther's complaints about the outhouse seat. You know Esther, Aggie's sister. Aggie, the one who married the Klutterhaus guy who lost two fingers that time at the sawmill? Anyway, Lars checked that outhouse up and down and could not for the life of him figure out why she was complaining. He finally told her that he had no idea what her problem was, so she said she'd just take him out there and show him. When he still couldn't see what the deal was, she told him to get right down there and look in the hole. Well, he did, but he still couldn't see anything. She said, 'Get down there farther. No, farther than that. Right down close to the hole.'

"Well, he did what he was told because he knew that he didn't have much of a choice. As he stood back up, a couple of the hairs of his beard caught in a little crack in that seat. Startled, he howled in pain like a hound with a treed raccoon in sight. 'Now do you see the problem?' Esther said. And she marched back to the house while Lars headed out to the barn to get some wood for a new seat."

I wondered earlier in these pages how many civil ribaldry stories are told so rarely that even though I have always been attentive and listened for them I must have missed some. Other stories, however, such as Lars and Esther's, are recited frequently and, despite the repetition, never fail to elicit a laugh from others who have probably heard them as often as I have, perhaps even earlier that same week. Or day.

Speaking of Treed Raccoons

As I have already noted, it is entirely possible that many jokes and stories, even though they fall within the rubric of civil ribaldry, report actual events or, at any rate, started with real events. It's not likely, but it's possible. Living in this small town and hearing rumors, gossip, and stories that I know for a fact are true certainly would support this observation. Sometimes, in fact, I have witnessed events that deserve retelling as humorous anecdotes, almost jokes, and I can also report that I have gleefully passed many of them along myself orally as well as in print.

For example, Kenny's son was about to marry a local girl and, as is the custom, had arranged for a bachelor party. As is also often the way here, the women had their own gathering in the house, tolerating if not understanding or encouraging what the men out in the barn were enjoying—namely, a stripper imported especially for the occasion from one of the baser establishments in a nearby city. At some point Kenny left his son and his young friends in the barn to share some special time with the dancer and returned to the house. When Kenny came in and greeted all the women in the house—his wife, his mother-in-law, other in-laws and in-laws to be, and neighbor ladies—Betsy, Kenny's wife, asked him how things were going with the stripper out in the barn. "Oh, fine," Kenny said with studied detachment. "You know how that goes. . . . It's fine for the young guys, but it sure doesn't mean that much to me anymore."

Betsy, just as calmly, said, "Before we go much further with this conversation, Kenny, you may want to wipe the whipped cream off your forehead."

Also a factual story, by my own witness, a local protective father always made sure his daughters were well sprinkled with sparkly glitter before he let them go out on a date with a young swain. That way, upon any couple's return home, all he had to do was glance out the front door's window as the date said his good-byes and see where the glitter had transferred to the young man to know exactly how much fun the evening had been.

Harvard Law

While I object to labeling the modern legend the *urban* legend, I have to admit that civil ribaldry does seem to be predominantly rural. It would be impossible to do a "scientific" survey or analysis proving or disproving that theory because, to begin with, of the difficulties I have noted earlier in collecting materials that are responses to casual and normal stimuli. My inference therefore is based on what appears in my narrow experience to be the most common content of the stories I class as civil ribaldry. One of my favorite examples is about an elderly man of my acquaintance who, as a young local, had studied hard in the public school in Dannebrog and confidently traveled east to take the entrance exams for Harvard Law School. (Now I'd heard about his history; he was more than usually intelligent but not, I think, the sort of student recruited by Harvard.) He returned home confident that he had done his best even though he had been thrown off by the last question on the long and demanding exam, an essay question asking only, "What's what?" He made a stab at the essay but was crushed weeks later when he received an official rejection from the school of his dreams.

Being the persistent sort, however, he continued working on the farm while he renewed his studies, borrowing books from educated people in the community, visiting the library in town, buying what he could from catalogs delivered to his parent's rural home. And the next year he went back to

Cambridge, confident that he was much better equipped intellectually than he'd been the year before. Again the entrance exams were rigorous, but he was breezing right along when once again he turned to the last page to find that the final essay asked again, "What's what?" His heart fell, but he did what he could to make sense of the philosophical conundrum. But once again, weeks later he received a rejection letter from the Harvard admissions office.

Still not discouraged, the lad continued his labored studies while continuing to work on his parents' farm, reading well into the night every night, considering weighty problems even while sitting on the tractor seat, debating issues with Bessie while milking the cow. A third time he took the train east and once again launched into the entrance trials, this time easily slicing through the math, geography, literature, art, culture, and legal segments of the test and then once again slamming into the stone wall on the last page, where the same question appeared yet once again: "What's what?"

His spirit broken, the boy gave up his hopes and resigned himself to spending the rest of his life working on the family farm. While his dreams for a profession in law had been crushed, he was after all still a healthy young man, so one day he went up in the barn loft to throw some hay down for the cows and got to wrestling playfully with the hired girl. One thing led to another, and pretty soon they were rolling around in the loft. Somehow one of the lad's hands accidentally found its way into the young girl's overalls. Feeling something he sure had not ever felt before, the lad sputtered, "Wow! What's *this*?!"

The girl smiled and asked coyly, "What's *what*?"

Whereupon the lad sputtered, "Damn! If I had known that four years ago, today I'd be a senior in Harvard Law School!"

While this story features Harvard, a distinctly urban and

urbane item, and higher education, with a college education being a fairly recent common aspiration among the youth of the rural Plains countryside, the details of the home, cows, barn, hay, hired girl, and overalls suggest a rural context or even a rural origin for the narrative.

Someone told me another story, again agricultural in nature, as having happened to an identified man of my acquaintance, and it also deals with the topic of the ever-tempting and convenient, even if not always comely, hired girl. Said gentleman was once fooling around at the end of a cornfield with the hired girl when things really got serious. As the two girded, or perhaps more precisely ungirded, their loins for the task, the young lady said, "Merle, I think maybe you should tie one of those overall straps around your ankle."

"Why's that?" he asked.

"Because," she said, "we may not come back down the same furrow."

For reasons I can't figure out, that has to be one of the most evocative remarks I've ever heard or seen in print.

Even when marriage made the hired girl an honest woman, her reputation for earthy enthusiasm apparently endured. I met Butch Williams, a legendary house mover in central Nebraska, when he came to my land near Dannebrog and gave us an estimate on moving a large old house about five miles from the other side of the town to a new site here. I didn't know it at the time, but Butch was as famous for his humor and storytelling as he was for rearranging the architectural landscape of the region. As we worked out our plans for moving the house, Butch looked us over—I was a little older than fifty at the time, and Linda was thirty-two—and said, "You two remind me of the old-timer who married the hired girl, who was about half his age. He told her, 'Dear, whenever I'm out in the fields working and you feel like you need a little loving, just step out the back door and fire the shotgun and I'll come running." Butch paused here a moment for effect and then added, "Poor old fella died two weeks into pheasant season."

In turn his tale reminds me of a time when an elderly gent from whom I was collecting pioneer stories told me the story of his courtship and marriage to the woman who was sitting beside him. They had both come from Denmark to Wisconsin at about the same time but on different ships. Until he accumulated enough money to set out on his own, he worked for an established farmer as a hired hand, and he came to know and admire his future wife, the hired girl from a farm not many miles away. When the time came to move to new land in Nebraska, he decided to propose marriage. So he walked over to the neighbor's farm, asked to see the hired girl, and framed his proposal as diplomatically, if not romantically, as he could: "Olga, I know I'm not a very handsome man, but I'd like to ask you to marry me and come with me to Nebraska."

He said she replied, and I could see from her smile that he was telling the story correctly, "You betcha, Lars! I'll marry you and go to Nebraska. As for your looks, they don't matter that much. You'll be working out in the field most of the time anyway!"

The Western mind very much wants clear lines between things and definite boundaries around things, but in nature and reality, such lines do not always exist. Consider the stories here. Butch Williams's story about the old farmer with the young wife and the story about the naive young man and the more experienced hired girl lack the specificity of names and locations one might expect in a bit of oral history, and there is simply "the feeling" that the tale exists as a story, told on just such occasions as Butch's meeting Linda and me. Even while the first narrative was told to me as having happened to a mutual acquaintance, and it may have, its lack of specificity leads me to believe it is simply a folktale told for a laugh, not a piece of oral history mean to enlighten one's understanding of the local heritage.

However, the third tale about the young Danish couple and their brief and unadorned courtship I heard directly from the man in question as a first-person narrative. The laughs of his wife sitting nearby, nodding in agreement as she heard the family story probably for the hundredth time, seemed to validate the story as a bit of oral history, but it is not widely distributed (in fact, probably rarely if ever told by anyone but the gentleman who told it to me) and therefore not in the "folk mouth." Yet. Perhaps some day down the line the story will stir interest enough for other tellers and find appreciative audiences. But not yet. And in all honesty I doubt that it will. But that doesn't detract in the least from the pleasure that the old gent got from telling me the story or that I had in hearing it.

Occasionally nominal examples of what I think of as "civil ribaldry" show up in more formal, sophisticated contexts such as *Playboy* magazine's "Party Joke" section, where the question might arise, do the jokes move from this popular culture distribution into oral, folk transmission, or has the process been the reverse, moving from informal, oral circulation into print? Without direct information from the publisher, which is not available, one can only guess, and my guess is the latter. The basis for that conclusion is that in print the stories are clumsy, rigid, cold, and frankly neither funny nor even interesting. That is, their modality seems to be oral transmission, or based on performance rather than print. And the stories lose something when published rather than told. I hope that isn't the case as I present such stories here, wrenched from the folk mouth and forever embalmed in ink on paper!

As I noted before, the idea of origins in traditional materials has always been a point of interest and contention, from the basic consideration of individual, idiosyncratic creation to a kind of collective polishing in the very act of transmission that defines what is and is not folklore. Are traditional stories that appear over incredibly wide geographic and historical distances a product of polygenesis—that is, individual inventions that are similar or even identical because of the consistency of human experience, intellect, and expression—or does a story (or proverb or recipe or technological development like smelting or log construction) originate with one inventive stroke of genius and then diffuse over centuries or millennia over those wide distances? There is evidence to support both theories.

I would argue, however, that we can determine in some cases at least a likely context for these stories of civil ribaldry from internal evidence. We can surmise with some good reason, for example, that the following story, depending on a knowledge of lutefisk, comes from a community familiar with Scandinavian foodways.

Two guys are talking out in front of the general store when one points to the other's dog and says, "Look there, Lars. Your dog must have worms because he's licking his ass."

And Lars says, "No, Ole, he's been eating lutefisk, and he's trying to get the taste out of his mouth."

Many of the stories in this collection contain elements that are clearly agricultural and, as often as not, techniques that precede modern, high-tech farming, or they include details that indicate a context of a small town. That is, the very nature of the stories per se suggests where they are most at home. As I argue here, I believe they are largely of rural origin and increasingly of the past. We certainly can identify some stories too as being of different origins, although they do exhibit the subtlety of diction and performance. For example, two stories have crossed my desk in the past two weeks that are clearly modern, probably urban, and more a product of cyberlore than of folklore. The very fact that they "crossed my desk," which is to say, appeared on my computer screen in the form of emails, affirms that suggestion.

In the first one, a man received the following text from his neighbor: "I am so sorry, Bill. I've been riddled with guilt, and I have to confess. I have been tapping your wife day and night when you're not around. In fact, more than you do. I'm not getting any at home, but that's no excuse for my behavior. I can no longer live with the guilt, and I hope you will accept my sincere apology and my promise that it won't happen again."

Bill, anguished, went into his bedroom, grabbed his gun, and without a word shot and killed his wife.

A few moments later a second text came in: "Damn Auto-Correct! I meant 'Wi-Fi,' not 'wife.'"

The term "tapping" alone narrows the time and geography of this story; I have never heard the term in oral circulation here in rural America, only in print or on television. What's even more restrictive is the technology that forms the basis of the story: texting, AutoCorrect, and Wi-Fi. Without those elements there is no story. It makes better sense in print; it's not a story that is easily *told.* I suspect the majority of my contemporaries wouldn't understand the story even if it was written, as it is clearly a product of the cyber generation.

Similarly the following story has been making the rounds over the past couple years, both in print and in oral narrative: An Arizona couple, both partners well into their eighties, goes to a sex therapist's office. The doctor asks, "What can I do for you?"

The man says, "Will you watch us have sexual intercourse?"

The doctor raises his eyebrows, but he is so amazed that such an elderly couple is asking for sexual advice that he agrees. When the couple finishes, the doctor says, "There's absolutely nothing wrong with the way you have intercourse." He wishes them good luck, charges them $50, and says good-bye.

The next week the same couple returns and asks the therapist to watch them again. The doctor is puzzled but agrees. This same thing happens several weeks in a row: the couple makes an appointment, has intercourse with no apparent problems, pays the doctor, and leaves. After three months of this routine, the doctor finally says, "I'm sorry, but I have to ask, just what is it you two are trying to find out?"

The man says, "We're not trying to find out anything. She's married, so we can't go to her house. I'm married, so we can't go to my house. The Holiday Inn charges ninety-eight dollars, and the Hilton charges a hundred thirty-nine. We do it here for fifty, and best of all, Medicare pays forty-three dollars of it!"

Again the content of the narrative suggests a modern origin: sex therapist, Holiday Inn, Hilton, Medicare . . . And the prices of accommodations are certainly not those of fifty years ago! It's not easy to imagine how a tale such as this one could have arisen in an older, rural context or how it could be adapted now to that format. It is a recent, urban story, plain and simple.

Another story that might fit neatly into the format of civil ribaldry but that clearly shows modern, if cross-generational, elements was widely told around here. It was clumsily put in print some years ago.

An elderly woman is on a trip and complains to the flight attendant that she has somehow gotten a sliver in her finger. The attendant tries to help her extract the irritant with tweezers but without success. Finally the elderly woman asks the flight attendant if she happens to have a bottle of apple cider in the galley. She does and takes it to the woman's seat. The woman opens the bottle, pours some into a cup on her tray table, and begins soaking her finger in the cider. The attendant, ever interested in ways to meet such emergencies, asks where the woman learned this interesting way of dealing with a splinter.

The woman explains that she learned it when her granddaughter was visiting during a break from college. She had overheard her talking to a friend on the telephone, saying that the night before, she had had a prick in her hand but it was much better once it was in cider.

The flight attendant, wisely concluding that discretion is the better part of a lot more than valor, moved on to serve cocktails to the people in first class.

Urban v. Rural

If a character from the city or a bearer of urbanity in a more general sense appears in civil ribaldry, he or she is often portrayed as the butt of the humor and clearly deemed the innocent in a context of rural sophistication . . . rural but sophisticated nonetheless. A dupe or victim of a tale may be rural, but in that event he is usually the victim of yet another rural or agricultural perpetrator. For example, a cowboy confronts a city visitor to the West over his fancy duds. The visitor protests, "Good man, I'll have you know that I am the son of a lord!"

The cowboy spits, "Out here sons of lords and sons of bitches are pretty much held in the same esteem."

In another, a farmer encounters a farmer friend coming out of the bank. "Man," he says, "if things get any worse in this economy, I'm going to rob this bank."

"If things get any worse," his friend says while waving a loan agreement, "I just *did* rob this bank."

The "Arkansas Traveler" is an excellent example of the elusiveness of a folk identity for any particular item. The vignette first appeared in the mid-nineteenth century with various people declaring authorship, and some had precise stories of how they came upon the idea. Perhaps the most accurate of these anecdotes are those in which the "author" claims to have been the "traveler" in question and to have encountered or participated in the repartee that characterizes the performance (a "skit," or clearly a performance) with alternative exchanges between a sharpster–country fiddler (or, in later versions, a banjo player) and a traveling carpetbagger, or city slicker. In the scenario the local is seated on the porch of his ragged cabin, playing a tune on a fiddle or banjo, when the traveler stops to ask directions.

TRAVELER: Howdy, Farmer. Is Little Rock down this road?

FARMER: All kinds of rocks down this road, big and little. [*Farmer plays first half of the tune "Arkansas Traveler" and does so between* each *exchange.*]

TRAVELER: No, I mean does this road *go* to Little Rock?

FARMER: Lived here a lot of years and the road ain't gone nowhere.

TRAVELER: Sure a lot of rocks around here. Where'd they all come from?

FARMER: Glacier brung 'em.

TRAVELER: Where'd the glacier go?

FARMER: Went back for more rocks.

TRAVELER: Your corn looks mighty yellow this year.

FARMER: Planted the yeller kind.

TRAVELER: I mean the corn don't look so good.

FARMER: Truth to tell, that corn don't look at all. It's the 'taters that got the eyes.

TRAVELER: So how did your 'taters turn out this year?

FARMER: Didn't turn out. We had to dig 'em.

TRAVELER: Can't you see your roof is leaking? Why don't you fix it?

FARMER: Can't fix it because it's raining.

TRAVELER: Then why don't you fix it when it's *not* raining?

FARMER: 'Cause then it's not leaking.

TRAVELER: Lived here all your life, have you, Farmer?

FARMER: Not yet.

TRAVELER: Not much difference between you and a fool, is there, Farmer?

FARMER: Just the porch rail and the fence.

TRAVELER: No, I mean you're not very smart.

FARMER: I ain't lost.

TRAVELER: Why don't you play the rest of that tune?

FARMER [*greatly excited*]: Why, you mean to say you know the rest of that song? You get right on up here, sit down, grab that banjo, take a pull on the jug, and show me how the rest of that dang song goes. Don't worry about gettin' to Little Rock. Tomorrow when the sun comes up, I'll hitch up the mule and take you there myself in my old wagon. And we can play that tune all the way there and back. Yes, sir! And now pass the jug this way while you show me the rest of that song.

[*The men play both stanzas of the tune.*]

While I suspect the tune and accompanying tale first circulated as a folktale or performance, the vignette has been performed in minstrel shows, in movies, on television, and almost surely at Boy Scout camps and high school drama exercises. Adaptions appeared as the state song of Arkansas and in paintings of the imagined scene. So is it folklore, popular culture, sophisticated art, primitive art? The best answer is yes. It has been all of those things and possibly still is being memorized and performed somewhere, at some level of sophistication, at this very moment. As noted earlier in my discussion of the character of folklore, the Arkansas Traveler is dynamic, vital, and adaptive. It's a good entertainment, and after almost two centuries in our culture at multiple levels, there's not a doubt in my mind that it lives on somewhere.

The moral of the story, other than that a good tune soothes the savage breast, is that neither party is quite as ignorant of things worth knowing as the other presumes. It is a suitable parable for all times. Another moral might be that that the rural bumpkin sitting on his front porch may not be as dull witted as you think. Or perhaps his apparent lack of understanding is simply another way of thinking. I've had and heard similar exchanges here in my own rural setting.

> ME: I heard you've planted strawberries already. Think you'll get any this first year?
>
> RURAL WORTHY: Probably not. I'll be too busy growing strawberries.

> ME: Hey, Bruce, how come a guy as ugly as you has such a good-looking daughter?
>
> RURAL WORTHY: I didn't do it with my face.

Overheard at the Dannebrog lumberyard:

> CUSTOMER: Hey, Bob, I need a two-by-four.
>
> BOB: How long?
>
> CUSTOMER: Quite a while. I'm building a garage.

In fact, I find that many of the most negative things I've heard about this tiny village I've adopted as a hometown come from the very people who live here. Further, they might not be insults at all but jokes that more likely express the coherence of the community than any genuine discomfort in it. For example, some are fond of saying, "It's said that if you have a hammer in Dannebrog, you're a carpenter. If you own the hammer, you're a contractor."

> VISITOR: What do people in Dannebrog do for a living?
>
> LOCAL: We're mostly in iron and steel. The women iron and the men steal.

Some have said of several old-time residents, "He came here thirty years ago with a ten-dollar bill and the Ten Commandments, and he hasn't broken either one since."

The Eternal Cuckold

While folktales I label civil ribaldry are not without widely held racial, religious, gender, and ethnic stereotypes—those too are part of traditional folklore after all!—it is my impression from looking at these materials over the years that they are more often than not self-deprecatory. If anything, a dominant (although not a universal) characteristic is that the content is self-deprecatory. Even the dialogue of the Arkansas Traveler demonstrates that the city man—and, for that matter, the country fiddler—is not as bright as he thinks he is, for he knows only half of the song, after all. A prevailing mood of civil ribaldry is human frailty.

Nothing is more endearing in humor than self-deprecation, joking about one's own failings and weaknesses. Most modern humor is anthropological, offering commentary on the peculiarities of our own and other cultures, but watching any stand-up comedian will quickly confirm that turning the barbs of humor inward is a sure way to win over an audience. The same is true with civil ribaldry.

Lunchbox, a local who as indicated by his nickname is a substantial figure of a man, had lost some weight. I noted that this change was probably really good for his health and maybe even his sex life, and he replied, "Yeah. I discovered two inches I didn't even know I had." I can't imagine a circumstance either where Lunchbox could have delivered that line before or where he would have heard it before. My guess is that it was his invention and utterly spontaneous.

An unlikely but not contrived context for such wit occurred during an early morning when I was sitting in the village tavern conversing with Eric, who then was its owner, as he did his weekly mopping of the floor. On the back band of his underwear as he bent to wring the mop, I noticed some small lettering—an M and, then a bit distanced from it, a Y. I chuckled and said, "Good grief, Eric, don't tell me you have underwear for every day and that one says 'Monday!'"

"Nope," he said. "May."

As I've said, my father, deaf from childhood, was a repository for jokes about deafness. In my own old age, as I found myself increasingly afflicted with the maladies of seniority, I wrote and published my book *Golden Years My Ass*, a litany of my own medical adventures. Such revelations are not complaints begging for pity but rather signals that one is dealing quite well with whatever problems have come along with the years.

A husband whose status as a cuckold is well established becomes the butt of jokes or even of conversations about the disgrace. As it quickly becomes clear even to a newcomer and outsider as I was, though, one is careful not to tell stories of cuckoldry while the injured party is present for fear that he indeed knows the pain of his situation, and his compatriots want to do what they can to avoid inflicting further injury. Exchanges of such stories can be seen therefore almost as reassurances that those in present company are safe and that no one knows anything that might hurt others in the circle. Perhaps that is why stories of conjugal infidelity, such as the following, are so widespread and so enthusiastically enjoyed.

While rummaging through his wife's dresser drawers looking for something or other, a farmer discovered a small cup containing three soybeans and $24 in cash. The collection was peculiar enough that the farmer asked his wife about it, and she sheepishly confessed, "Over the years, dear, I haven't been completely faithful to you. But on those occasions when I have had dalliances, I put a soybean in that cup to remind me of my indiscretion."

The farmer was a bit shaken but admitted that he hadn't always been faithful either, so he was inclined to forgive his wife and forget these few moments of weakness in his wife's marriage vows. After all, three lapses aren't that bad in an eighteen-year marriage, he figured. "I'm curious though," he went on. "I understand the three soybeans, but where did the twenty-four dollars come from?

"Oh, that," the wife replied. "Well, when soybeans hit eight dollars a bushel, I sold."

The motif of the unfaithful wife who keeps accounts is in fact a constant theme in bedroom humor.

Not saving enough of the egg money to keep the family going, a husband and wife decide that one way for them to make the mortgage and maybe even save up a little extra would be to place a fruit jar under their bed, and after each time they have sex, the wife will drop a quarter into the jar. One day the husband is looking for a lost shoe under the bed and discovers the jar . . . stuffed with bills . . . fives, tens, and even a few twenties . . . and with a couple of quarters down at the bottom. "What's this all about?" he asks his wife, thinking that maybe he's been a little more active than he thought. Or maybe that his wife had been picking up some spare change on her own along the way. "We agreed to put a quarter in the jar every time we made love, but what's with all the paper money?"

"Do you think everyone's as cheap as you?" the wife asks coyly.

And similarly a married couple decides that the only way they can make ends meet is for the wife to do a little extra business now and then while the old man is out in the fields. So she puts the word out around town that she'd be interested in entertaining some of the local gents when the coast was clear and that they should check in with her and "talk business," as it were. She then suggests to her husband that maybe he should spend some time out in the fields so they can get caught up on some bills. For a couple of days he makes it generally known that he'll be out working in the fields pretty early until pretty late. After the week is over, he decides to see how the extra business is going and asks his wife what the ledger looks like. She reaches into her dresser drawer and hauls out a cigar box with $60.25 in it.

"Who was the cheapskate who gave you the quarter?" the husband asks.

"They all did," she replies.

Again and again in such situations it is the woman who is clever and the male who is duped. The motif is deep in the human psyche because within such human turmoil, the identity of the mother of a child is never in question, but the father's may often be. Such is the nature of mankind and biology, and such is the nature of humor.

When our daughter Antonia was yet to be born, we read a letter in a newspaper advice column from a man who was wondering about something his wife had told him. While he was of Swedish descent and his wife of German heritage, they had just had their first child, and the baby was clearly African American. His wife had explained to him that every fifth child born into this world is black, and it was simply their turn. And he was wondering if this was indeed the case. I laughed at the letter and handed the newspaper to Linda, whereupon she said, "Welsch, if this baby of ours turns out to be black, you'll have a lot of explaining to do." I laughed. Kind of.

When Antonia was born and grew through childhood

and into a woman, she wound up being absolutely identical to my daughter from a previous marriage. Linda said, "Sometimes I look at Antonia and Joyce, and they look so much alike, I wonder if I am really Antonia's mother."

The motif of the cuckold is universal in both traditional lore from the folk mouth and idiosyncratic humor from individual comic geniuses. A classic story based on this very human tension appears in many folktale collections in many variations. The next one is from my files.

A boy wants to marry a girl from a farm not far away, but the boy's father takes him aside in the barn one day and tells him, "Son, I have to tell you something. I confess that I slept with that girl's mother a few times about the time you came along, and to tell you the truth, there is some real chance that you and that girl are brother and sister."

Of course, the lad is heartbroken, so he goes to his mother for advice. "Don't you fret none about Emmy Lou being your sister," the mother reassures the boy with a wink. "Maybe she is . . . but you ain't her brother."

In another example along the same theme, a father teases his three boys about the two having hair black as pitch while the third has flaming red hair. "I must have had some rust in the old cannon," he chuckles.

The redheaded boy is on the verge of tears when his mother comes out and comforts him, saying, "Oh now, come on, Little Jeb. Them other two would have been as redheaded as you if we hadn't gotten so far behind in the rent."

Along these same lines, Sam and Becky are celebrating their fiftieth wedding anniversary, and Sam asks a question.

SAM: So, Becky, I was wondering . . . Have you ever cheated on me?

BECKY: Oh Sam, why would you ask such a question now? You really don't want to ask a question you don't want to hear the answer to.

SAM [*curious*]: Yes, Becky, I really want to know, please. Have you ever been unfaithful to me?

BECKY [*struggles a moment*]: Well, all right. Yes, I have cheated on you. But only three times.

SAM: Three times . . . Hmmm, well, when did they happen?

BECKY: Well, Sam, do you remember when you were thirty-five years old and you really wanted to start the business on your own and no bank would give you a loan? And do you remember, then one day the bank president himself came over to the house and signed the loan papers, no questions asked? Well . . .

SAM: Oh, Becky, you did that for me? I respect you even more than ever, knowing you would do such a thing for me! So when was the second time?

BECKY: Well, Sam, do you remember when you had that heart attack and you needed open-heart surgery and knowing our finances, no surgeon wanted to take on the job? And do you remember how the doctor eventually came all the way from the city to do the surgery himself, and then you were all well and as good as new in a matter of weeks? Well . . .

SAM: Oh, my goodness!! Becky, how wonderful that you would do such a thing for me, to save my life! I can't believe your love. I couldn't have a more wonderful wife. I am so moved by your devotion! So, all right then—when was that third time you cheated on me?

BECKY: Well, Sam, do you remember a few years ago, when you really wanted to be president of the church congregation? And you were forty-seven votes short?

Now's Your Chance

Early in my work with pioneer stories and sod-house life, a sweet little old lady told me a story, and the thought that she was not being entirely truthful would never have occurred to me at the time. At least not until she had finished her story. She told me that her father was an itinerant household goods salesman in the years of homesteading. He traveled from sod house to sod house, selling needles, thread, pots, spices, and other small goods that wouldn't merit what could require a day . . . or two days . . . of wagon or horseback travel to town to get and yet that a pioneer family would really need. And he made a pretty good living at that occupation, which was a common part of the frontier landscape.

He was once out on his remote rounds, however, when a ferocious blizzard hit unexpectedly, and he knew that he was in a life-threatening situation. It was not at all uncommon for people to die in such sudden storms, and this traveling drummer knew that he was in real trouble. Imagine then his relief when he came upon a small sod house and farmstead with lantern light streaming out the window and smoke coming out the chimney. He knew that he had probably just found his salvation.

He banged on the door of the soddie and was instantly pulled in out of the storm by the man of the house, who led the traveler to the stove and its warmth. Then the farmer went out and bedded down the traveler's horses in the small barn right alongside his own animals, feeding them oats just the same as if they'd been his own team. Such was the nature of frontier hospitality, after all. Back in the house they exchanged information about the goings on in the world and on the frontier. When time came for the evening meal, the wife apologized that they were poor folks and didn't have much to share by way of vittles, but of course the stranger was welcome to share in what they had. She took a large bowl of cottage cheese from her small cupboard and put it on the table. Each of the diners had a spoon with which they ate from that common bowl of cottage cheese. They had not eaten more than a couple spoonfuls of this modest fare when the woman rose up from her chair, picked up the bowl, and said, "That's all we have in the house to eat so we'd better make it last." She put the bowl back into the cupboard.

When time came for them to retire, again the hosts apologized. All they had by way of furniture in their hut was a single bed with a straw mattress and one quilt, so the three of them had to sleep there side by side: the woman on one side, the husband in the middle, and the traveler on the outside.

Not long after they had settled down and gone to sleep, they could hear above the howl of the storm and through the thick walls of that sod hut a horrendous uproar outside the house. The farmer jumped up out of bed and said, "The horses are fighting out in the barn!" He grabbed the lantern and his coat and went out through the cold wind and snowdrifts to the barn to separate the horses and the harnesses and to reestablish the peace. Well, he had no sooner gone out the door than the lady of the house reached over, gave the traveler a little poke, and said, "Now's your chance."

So he got up and ate the rest of the cottage cheese.

The sweet old lady who told me this story did so with great seriousness, convincing me until the punch line that she was indeed reciting a bit of family oral history. Then she smiled archly, winked, and seemed to bask in the warmth of having duped this young professor into taking her recitation seriously.

While we're on the subject of female constancy, the following story should get double billing: A hired girl goes to the lady of the house and says she thinks she should have a raise in her salary.

MRS. FAHNHAMMER [*surprised*]: Betsy, why do you think you should be getting more money?

BETSY: Well, missus, there are three reasons why I should be getting more money. First off, I do a better job with the laundry and ironing than you do.

MRS. FAHNHAMMER: And just where did you get that idea, young lady?

BETSY: Your husband, Mr. Fahnhammer, told me so.

MRS. FAHNHAMMER: Oh, he did, did he?

BETSY: And the second reason is that I'm a better cook than you are.

MRS. FAHNHAMMER: Nonsense. Who told you such a thing?

BETSY: Your husband, Mr. Fahnhammer said so.

MRS. FAHNHAMMER: Hmmm, well . . .

BETSY: And the third reason is, I'm better in bed than you are.

MRS. FAHNHAMMER: Really! And I suppose Mr. Fahnhammer told you that too then, did he?!

BETSY: No. Bob, the hired man, told me that.

MRS. FAHNHAMMER: How much do you think you should be paid?

Efforts to reignite the fires of romance in a marriage may not always turn out to be the best solution either, however. A farm wife gets to thinking about how good her old man has been to her over the years and how little appreciation she has shown for his support, so she decides to get things on the right track again. She dresses up in a slinky see-through outfit she had ordered for the occasion from a catalog sent in a plain wrapper. Then she lights a couple of scented candles, cools down a six-pack of his favorite beer, cooks him his favorite meal of liver and onions, puts satin sheets on the bed, and sprinkles on a little of the most seductive foo-foo water she has in her inventory.

When the old man arrives home from the tavern, considerably worse for the wear, she welcomes him in, takes off his shoes, brings him his beer, feeds him the liver and onions, and rubs his shoulders. Finally she invites him to the bedroom for "a special treat." As she pulls him to the bed, she asks if there is anything he wants. "Anything at all?"

"What the hell," he shrugs. "I might as well. I'll catch hell when I get home anyway."

Using the Imagination

Cuckoldry, betrayal, the hired man, un-missionary postures, humiliation, indignation—it's hard to imagine how such a combination can still be handled subtly if not delicately, but somehow in the genre of civil ribaldry it seems accomplished. It is in fact a perfectly natural, so to speak, marriage. For one thing, despite all we might want to think, sex is funny. If you doubt me, just think about it a bit. Bring some images to your mind. It's funny. Second, the noun in the name I have given the genre is "ribaldry," a slightly more civil term for, well, uh, *sex*. Third, as I discuss in greater detail in the following material, the stories I am examining and sharing with you come primarily from and persist in rural and middle to lower classes. The curiosity is not so much that sexual topics and entanglements dominate the genre but that they are not only dealt with in a relatively genteel manner but also couched in humor. What has come to be a serious and even forbidden topic in formal and high-class culture in American society was and to some degree still is perfectly natural within folk culture.

The following two, um, innocent examples, one imagines, can be told in mixed or sensitive company, even with children present, without rousing much more than their puzzlement. As prurience is in the mind of the listener, the only protest might come from the knowing adult listeners, who can either smile and let the ribaldry pass or laugh and reveal their awareness.

A city fellow was looking for a butcher hog of some particulars and was directed to the farm of Ol' Jeb. He found Jeb out in the pig sty and told him exactly what he wanted: "Yes, my fine fellow, I am looking for a pig of about 220 pounds, not too fat, not too small."

"Fine," said Jeb. "That sure won't be a problem." He looked over his stock, put his eye on one sow, and strolled over to her. In one swoop he grabbed that pig by the tail, put the tail in his teeth, and lifted her from the ground. "Noop," he mumbled through his clenched teeth still holding that hog up off the ground. "This un's closer to 200." He released that hog and cast his eye around the hog lot. Spotting another, he grabbed it by the tail and again lifted it from the ground with his teeth. "Noop, this un's more like 230. We cun do bedder." With that he released the pig and started his search for another. He grabbed a third hog, lifted it from the ground with his teeth, and smiled, "Yup . . . this is the un. Right at 222 pounds."

As you can imagine, the buyer watched this performance with complete amazement. "Are you telling me you can actually weigh hogs that way? Simply by hefting hogs up by the tail with your teeth?"

"You bet," said Jeb. "Done it that way all my life. Everyone in my family has the craft." Jeb waved at his boy Elmer, who was over at the other end of the lot, throwing ear corn into the hog pen. "Come here, boy. I need you to weigh this hog and check my figures for me."

So the kid grabbed that last hog and lifted it up in his teeth. He grimaced through his clenched jaw, "Okay, Pap. I'd estimate this un at somewhere between 220 and, oh, maybe 224 pounds."

"That is truly amazing," said the prospective buyer. "But

how do I know you two didn't set this up beforehand just to bamboozle me?"

Jeb laughed and said, "Oh, lots of people are surprised when we weigh hogs like this, and almost all of them have their doubts about whether we can do it or not. But I can prove our accuracy here. Son, run up to the house and get your mother to come down here a minute." And the kid goes hot-footing it off to the house up on the hill.

Pretty quick the kid comes running back and says, "Pap, Ma is busy and can't come down right now."

"Huh?" snorts the disappointed Jeb. "What is she so darned busy doing that she can't come down here and help me out with this customer?"

"Well, Pap, so far as I can tell she's weighing the hired man."

Such stories help explain why my friend Rick tells of the farmer who placed a newspaper ad for a hired man, stipulating he "must be over seventy years old." When asked why, the farmer explained, "I got an old tractor and a young wife, and I don't want nobody throwing a rod in either one of 'em."

Speaking of rods, a couple of old-timers named Ben and Ralph were out hunting deer, and Ben was bragging about his brand new rifle and the state-of-the-art scope he'd mounted on it. "Just take a look through that thing," the proud marksman boasted. "You can see all the way down past that woodlot and right to my house with that thing."

Ralph took the rifle and had a look through the scope just as directed but hesitated a little long. Then he said uncertainly, "Uuuh, Ben, I can in fact see all the way to your house. And, well, I can see right into your bedroom window too. And, ummmm, I see your wife in there. And she's, er, stark naked. And I guess that's your hired man, Jimmy. And by damn, he's naked too . . ."

After an uncomfortable silence, Ben muttered angrily to Ralph, "While you got that thing sighted in, why don't you just shoot my wife's head off and put an end to that business? And then pop Jimmy right in his old Johnson bar to teach *him* a lesson too."

After another uncomfortable pause, Ralph observed quietly, "Well, Ben, appears it'll only take one cartridge."

Ways of the Wise

Perhaps too indelicate for a general audience but nonetheless still in this line of stories of revealing indiscretions, one of the most widely told stories I've heard in central Nebraska concerns the smart-alecky husband who, upon crawling into bed beside his young wife, pats her on the fanny and laughs, "You know, if that thing got busy laying eggs, we could get rid of the chickens. Hahaha!" Since he thought that was so funny, he extended the image and patted her breasts too, laughing, "And if these things got to going, we could get rid of the milk cow."

The humor ended, however, when the young wife patted the old man on *his* private parts and smiled, "And if this thing got up and went to work, we could get rid of the hired man."

An important part of civil ribaldry highlights sophistication not only from the rural bumpkin, as in the case of the Arkansas Traveler, but also from an unexpected source: the aged, women, and children. When the element of surprise comes from a protagonist who is both elderly *and* female, the humor is redoubled.

For instance, an elderly woman is asked by a health practitioner if she's been bedridden before, and she replies proudly, "Bed ridden?! Why, yes, hundreds of times. And twice in a buggy!"

While watching young people dancing and expressing some dismay at the exhibition, another older woman is asked, "So then, Granny, do you remember the minuet?" And she replies, "The men I et? Hell, I can't even remember all of them I screwed!"

Nor is sophistication limited to the elderly. When a pregnant young woman who is, uh, well, very popular with the local boys appears before a judge, she asks for child support for the baby she is clearly carrying. The judge asks her, "Do you know for sure who the father is?"

She answers quite logically, "For heaven's sake, Your Honor, if you ate a can of beans, would you know which one made you fart?"

An important part of humor is surprise, as in the sudden appearance of the unexpected—for example, a child or an old lady or a young lady who is not as innocent as one expects, a rural rube with unanticipated sophistication, or a city man or woman of the world with remarkable naïveté.

A teacher welcomes her young students back to the classroom after their summer vacations and asks them to report on what they did over their summer months. Suzie says she went to her uncle Marvin's farm. In the barn she helped him milk the cows, but while carrying the bucket of fresh milk back to the house, she stumbled and spilled the entire lot into the dirt of the yard. But her kind uncle comforted her and, wiping away her tears, told her not to be upset because the next day Bessie would give them another pailful.

The teacher, hoping to make a moral lesson of the experience, asked, "And what did you learn from that, Suzie?"

"Not to cry over spilled milk."

"That's right, dear. And Homer, what did you do this summer while school was out?"

"Well, I went to my uncle Charlie's farm."

The teacher asked, "And what did you do while you were there?"

"Aunt Em sent me out to gather the eggs. But when I was walking back to the house, I stumbled and every one of those eggs fell on the ground and broke. But Auntie Em told me not to cry because the next day we'd go back out to the henhouse and find that those chickens had laid another whole supply that we could be more careful with."

"And what did you learn from that, Homer?" the teacher asked.

"We shouldn't put all our eggs in one basket."

"That's right. Good for you and good for your aunt Em. Little Willy, what did you do all summer?"

Willy replied, "Well, Teacher, I went to my grandpa's farm."

"And what did you do there?"

"Mostly we sat around, and Grandpa told us stories about when he was in the war."

"Oh, that's interesting," the teacher said. "What kind of stories did he tell?"

"He said he was down in his foxhole one day when all at once them Germans came charging over the hill. He knew he was in plenty hot water, because all he had with him in that foxhole was a bottle of that Jack Daniels whiskey, six bullets, two hand grenades, and a bayonet. Those Germans came running right straight at him, so Grandpa drank down that entire bottle of Jack Daniels whiskey. He killed six German with his last six bullets. Then here came six more Germans, and he killed them with his two hand grenades. When six more came running over the hill, Grandpa pulled out his bayonet and stabbed all six of them, saving the day for the entire American Army."

"Wow, Willy, that is some story. And what did you learn from that?"

"Don't screw around with Grandpa when he's been drinking."

And occasionally we find narratives describing the epiphany of discovery.

There were two old maid sisters who wouldn't have anything to do with men. They seemed to think that men were just about the worst things on earth. They wouldn't even let their female cat out of the house for fear she would suffer "a fate worse than death" at the carnal lust of one of the local alley tomcats. But somehow one of the spinsters eventually met a nice gent at a church tent meeting, became friendly with him, and darned if she didn't finally up and marry him. After the wedding they left on their honeymoon, and a couple days later the other sister received a postcard from Niagara Falls saying only, "Let the cat out."

By far and away the most popular topic of rumor and gossip in the rural countryside centers on precisely this kind of extra-social activity. I detected this notion early in my residence in Dannebrog when I was in our village grocery store, and the child of a woman of notorious repute came in, picked up some small items, and said to Ray Johnson, the store's proprietor, "Charge these to my daddy."

Ray, knowing the child and her mother well, winked at me and asked her laconically, "And who might that be?"

One can't help but think of an occasion when this selfsame shopkeeper was reportedly dealing with a father of one of the local large and expanding Danish families. The man was buying groceries and mentioned to Ray that he and his wife had had yet another child, another boy . . . their eleventh with nary a daughter. "So," Ray said by way of casual conversation, "you got yourself a boy every time then?"

And the rural gent said, "No, Ray, actually there's some times we don't get nothing at all."

A rural home has only a few regular visitors, so it's not surprising that if cuckoldry is the topic of a story the potential cast of characters is limited. Most days I see two people—my wife Linda and the postmaster when I retrieve our mail in town. Over the years and especially after hearing the following story, I have decided it is a good idea to have a mailbox at the post office and to go to town each day to retrieve the mail. One local reported proudly in the town café one day that his wife had to have some repair work done on her nether parts, and he boasted, "That's what happens when a woman has to deal with a fence-post peter." His brag quickly had cold water splashed on it when another man at the table remarked, "Huh. You must have the same mailman we do."

For another example with the same theme but with a fuller narrative:

A little boy has dreams that often and uncannily come true. One morning at breakfast he says, "Daddy, I dreamed last night that the dog died." His dad went out into the backyard and, sure enough, that dog was as dead as a doornail. The next morning the kid announces that he dreamed the cat died, and out in the barn the father finds the dead cat.

Then one morning the boy tells his father that he dreamed there was a terrible car wreck out on the road in front of the house and that his father died. All that day the father does everything he can to be careful, avoiding the road out in front of the house and keeping an eye out for anyone coming down that road when he is nearby.

As he comes in from the field on his tractor that night, he is a nervous wreck from worrying about the boy's dire omen of the morning. He flops down in his lounge chair, happy to still be alive. "Better get me a beer," he says to his wife. "I've had a terrible day."

"*You've* had a terrible day?!" She sputters. "I heard this terrible noise out on the road this morning, and when I went running out there, here was this terrible wreck and the mailman dead as a doornail in his delivery car."

Traffic Flow

Another of the characteristics of civil ribaldry that place the genre close to the legend is that it provides no signals that it is an artificial, fictional, or formulaic story that is being performed as something separate from normal, continuing conversation. The fairy tale has its classic opening and closing lines that everyone recognizes immediately—"once upon a time" and "they all lived happily ever after"—along with internal signals such as princes and princesses, witches and giants, occurrences predictably in threes, magical beings and events. Jokes often have the same kind of indicators—"a priest, a rabbi, and a Baptist minister walk into a bar"—or even a direct statement that a joke is about to be performed: "What's the difference between a . . . ," "knock, knock . . . ," "why does a Polack . . . ," "a blonde was driving down the street one day . . . ," and so on. Even the modern legend gives us hints about what we are going to hear in its introduction—for example, "a friend of my cousin's was in this tavern and . . ."—not to mention the manner in which its reporter tells it, using surprise, obvious excitement, and breathless wonder. No one confuses these clearly signaled narratives as gossip, news, or the performance of a standard folktale.

There are no such signals or segues with civil ribaldry. You can't tell when you are hearing one and in fact may have heard the complete story before realizing what it is. Or as has happened sometimes with me, I only realize days later what was actually being said in the story or the remark or that I actually was witness to a folktale. I think, for example, of the time I was sitting in the Dannebrog Tavern and talking with the barmaid, who is noted for her biting wit, when a friend came in and took the stool beside me. "Make it Old Taylor whiskey," he told the lady behind the bar, and without hesitation she said, "Make up your mind." I was embarrassed that I didn't laugh until three days later. I had not heard this line before. Only later did I learn it is a well-worn and smart-alecky line that barkeepers often use, but I completely missed the point at the time.

I should have seen it coming because this same salty woman was tending bar when a different friend came in at another time and said, as he sat down, "Anheuser Busch." And she replied, "Just great. And how's your peter?" Now those may be standard lines for barmaids . . . I wouldn't know, having never been one, but other experiences with this same woman in other circumstances suggest to me these responses may simply have been her way of demonstrating both her native wit and female expressions of civil ribaldry.

Speaking of female wit, I recall in particular when Linda and I sat with three couples together at the Big Table in the tavern, and the discussion turned to what path we would take if we lost our mates. I brought up the story about a time when I was in the hospital with severe cardiac problems, and a local told me later that he had seen Linda at the newspaper office in a nearby city, inquiring about the price of obituaries. He told me that the clerk informed Linda that obits cost $2 a word, but the first five words were free. So she said, "Okay, make it 'Rog died. Tractors for sale.'" When Linda heard that, she only elaborated on my penchant for collecting antique Allis-Chalmers tractors and asked around town what the protocol would be about placing the sale bill for the auction alongside my obituary.

And so our discussion went. Eventually it came to whether any of us would remarry should something happen to our spouse. The husband of the woman who sometimes tended bar got all huffy and said, "Kathy, I swear, if you ever marry again, I'm going to come back to haunt you and make your sex life miserable." To which Kathy said quietly, "The more things change, the more they stay the same." I cannot believe that that topic, in that kind of context, had come up before for this woman. She simply pulled the line out of her own creative mind.

By contrast, a story I've heard often enough around here that I believe I cannot honestly consider it as a result of one person's creative mind and quick humor but as a genuine "folk" tale in wider circulation tells of the fellow who is reading obituaries in the local newspaper. He looks up and remarks to his wife, "Honey, if I should die suddenly, I want you to sell all my stuff immediately."

"Why's that?" she asks.

"Because I don't want you marrying some other asshole who will use my stuff."

To which she says, "And what makes you think I'd marry another asshole?"

Here's a similar scenario with a not altogether different conclusion:

HUSBAND: If I were to die suddenly and you were to get married again, would you let your new husband drive my tractor?

WIFE [*comfortingly*]: Dear, I don't want to talk about such nonsense.

HUSBAND: Well, but if I died and you remarried, would you let the new guy use my favorite lounge chair here in the living room?

WIFE: I told you, honey, I don't even want to consider such a thing. So just forget about it.

HUSBAND: Well, it's been on my mind and is bothering me. If I died and you remarried, you wouldn't let this new guy play *my* banjo, would you?

WIFE: Dear, I told you. I do *not* want to talk about this kind of thing, so just forget it. Besides, . . . he's left-handed.

Speaking of the Innocence of the Gentler Sex

One of the reasons suggestive comments, stories, and jokes told by women are particularly remarkable and remarked upon is that they come from women. I think the common perception in many circles, and especially in the rural, lower-class, backwoods environment in which civil ribaldry flourishes, is that women are still imagined to be delicate flowers, the fair sex, the tender gender. I honestly believe some men are still of the mind that if a woman heard some of their usual language, humor, and stories, she would swoon away with a case of the vapors. Stories of civil ribaldry suggest otherwise. To a surprising degree . . . at least to my tender sensibilities . . . in these materials it is women who demonstrate the sophistication in bawdy matters and as often as not men who are the naifs.

The largest subcategory within the larger category of civil ribaldry deals with marital infidelity, cuckoldry, and the clueless male, and to my mind that is remarkable as primarily men tell these tales. The common element of the sexually sophisticated and charged women in the stories would seem to be unlikely, but, well, . . . here it is. Because of the language I have never thought of the following story as a good example of civil ribaldry, although it has been for many years one of my favorites . . . and perhaps is an indication of why it is also widely kept in oral circulation by other men.

For years a guy has looked for just the right woman to marry and has developed a little trick for determining if he has at long last found a woman of pure virtue and not just another wanton strumpet of the New Age. His test comes into play at that point when the relationship seems to have reached a moment of decision. At the right moment, the man opens his zipper, shows his pride and joy to the young lady he is considering to be his one-and-only bride, and asks, "What do you call this?"

If she uses one of the many crude terms for his member, that ends his courtship, and he moves on. His presumption is that he will eventually marry a beautiful, young woman innocent enough to meet his standards if he can find one who is shocked when she sees his "instrument" and gasps, "Why, I guess that's your pee-pee," or maybe "tinkler," or even better, "I have no idea what that is."

You can imagine how pleased the man is that after his long search he encounters a woman so innocent that she shuns the crude language of the street and instead uses a sweet term of innocent childhood when declaring upon seeing his organ, "Oh dear! That's a wee-wee!" So he proposes to her, she accepts, and they are married. But when the wedding is over and night falls over the newlyweds' bed, he again reveals himself and announces, "Dear, now that we are married and about to begin our long years together, I want to make one thing clear: from now on, you will refer to this as my *cock*, okay?"

"Oh, dear," she shrugs with a laugh, "I've seen plenty of cocks. And *that* is a wee-wee!"

Innocence is not always an asset in such situations.

A man married a young woman of genuine innocence and found that he had to explain to her what was expected of her on their conjugal couch: "Honey, when you feel that you'd like some loving, just reach over and tug on this, and I'll know what you have in mind."

The bride asked, "And what if I don't feel like I want any loving?"

"Then," the groom said, "just reach over and tug on it twenty-five times."

Another side of this apparently interminable search for elusive virginity (and why is it never a woman who looks for male innocence?) is reflected in a conversation between a father and son. The son explains to his father that these days, nice girls are few and far between, and he is at a loss to think of how to sort out the gold from the dross. His father says he should buy a can of green paint, and when things get to a point where a decision is about to be made and a trip to bed may be in the offing, he should paint his testicles green. When the lad asks what good this would do, the father says, "If she looks at that and says, 'Those are the strangest ones I've ever seen,' it may be time to move along."

Only yesterday Linda referenced an old bit of civil ribaldry when we were discussing a length of iron stock I was about to buy and needed to haul in her pickup truck. I said I would need 7½ feet and thought it would fit crosswise in the bed of her truck. All she had to say was "Well, Rog, you know how bad women are with measurements . . ." Her allusion, so indirect few others would understand what she was laughing at, was to the pretended riddle, "Do you know why women are so bad at measuring? All their lives they've been told that this"—and hold out your forefinger and thumb to a gap of about three inches—"is nine inches."

I admire but lack the kind of instant response Linda seems to pull out of nowhere and apparently as much to her surprise as to mine. This past spring I noted that Ash Wednesday was coming up, and as I have done for years, I proposed giving up for Lent cold, lumpy gravy . . . a standard, trite, and by now, no-longer-funny remark. When I asked her what she would be sacrificing, she said, "Sex." When I expressed my surprise (and dismay!), she reassured me, "Oh, don't worry, Rog. Only in town!" I did a spit take, and she recoiled in obvious embarrassment at what had come out of her own mouth. For her, what I think is genius comedic invention is as natural and irrepressible as a sneeze.

The topic of women's humor, especially about sex and marriage, are found in several places throughout this book because I find it particularly interesting that men generally seem to think that women have no culture of humor and most certainly not about sex, rarely about marriage, and never when men are the butts of the joke. Not so. I think that field is very vast and offers rich rewards for the researcher, but I don't think it's going to be a male who opens the treasury. Or understands it once it is uncovered.

A woman sitting at a table sipping a glass of wine with her husband suddenly says, to his surprise, "I love you so much, I don't think I could live without you."

Her husband smiles and says, "Is that you or the wine talking?"

She says quietly, "It's me . . . talking to the wine."

On another note, the two ideas of failing male capacities with old age and surprising sophistication and experience on the part of women combine to form one of the most prominent elements of the body of tales classified as civil ribaldry. The clueless couple, the clueless male, and less frequently the clueless female are common themes of civil ribaldry.

A family had baby after baby, year after year, and the town's observation was that they must "be playing a lot of sheet music" or maybe the rumor was true that this innocent couple believed it was the light that was attracting all those kids. Then the string of children stopped suddenly. The general opinion was that the population explosion was finally brought to a stop when the man of the family put up a big sign saying "Absolutely No Salesmen!" and moved the mailbox to the other end of the lane.

At least that seems a wiser course than what another couple did. After having more children than they could handle, the couple decided that the man of the family should probably start sleeping out in the barn. And his wife agreed that if that worked in controlling their population explosion, then she would move out there too.

Bruce Davis, now gone from the storytellers' circle here, once admitted that the words he had used to propose to his wife Annette were, "You're what?!" He also maintained that on their first date he had asked Annette if she would scream for help if he tried to kiss her. Her reported response: "Only if I think you need it."

Oh, Dat Ole! Oh, Dat Lena!

A popular modern form of civil ribaldry and other sorts of folk humor such as the pretended riddle, pretended obscene riddle, and so forth, feature the Ole and Lena stories. Especially strong in the Dakotas, Wisconsin, and Minnesota, they are cherished and recited with special glee, as an example of America's affection for self-deprecation would have it, by Scandinavians! Folklore is a living, ever-changing form of culture. So the favored ethnic slur has changed over the years from the Irishmen Pat and Mike to the Germans Hans and Fritz to the minstrel Rastus to the Czech Lumir to the Hispanic or Latino Pedro and then to Ole and Lena. There are always protests about such insulting stories and bafflement when they are merrily told by those who would appear to be the butt of the jokes. One way we learn about the common man's awareness about the nature of folklore and the degree of its offensiveness is through "meta-folklore"—that is, folklore about folklore. In this case, we're talking about ethnic slurs about ethnic slurs: What is black and blue and red all over? An Irishman who's been telling Polack jokes on Pulaski Avenue. (Or as heard around here, "in Loup City," Nebraska's "Polish capital.") And in this area of Nebraska, where the local citizen of Teutonic origins gets a "square head"—that is, a box, not a bowl—haircut, you might hear, "He's so German that he carries a cigar box with him when he goes to the barber shop."

Nor are all the cross-national barbs shot from the mainstream toward a minority. I was told the following story in central Nebraska, where Scandinavian populations abound.

A Norwegian comes home so drunk that he collapses into the pigpen, where he rolls around in the muck and mire, finally winding up lying alongside the old sow. Besodden, he throws his arm around the sow and asks, "Er du svensk?" (Are you Swedish?)

"Norsker (Norwegian)," grunts the pig. "Norsker!"

How targeted and insulting are Ole and Lena stories? We can determine that from how many of the stories are told to us by Swedish, Norwegian, and Danish Americans. And from stories such as the following one, which of course a Danish American shared with me. And excuse the dialect, but I have found that for some reason these particular stories are *always* told in an exaggerated, thoroughly artificial Scandinavian accent.

A preacher told an Ole and Lena joke from the pulpit as a way of getting his congregation into the mood for his more serious sermon, but after the service one of his flock expressed his unhappiness with his choice of butts for his ethnic humor. The parishioner explained that his own grandparents were pioneering immigrants who came to this nation from Sweden and faced untold hardships to give their family a solid foothold in the New World. Insulting Ole and Lena stories, he observed, seemed quite inappropriate, especially when a clergyman tells them and from the pulpit, no less.

The preacher replied, "But, you know, I really think these Ole and Lena stories are very funny. I like hearing them and telling them, and everyone in my congregation seems to enjoy them too."

"I understand that," the offended party said. "I enjoy them too. But to avoid insulting my family members or any other people around me, what I do when I want to tell one of these stories is to couch it in biblical terms, so it becomes almost a religious parable. The next time you want to tell a joke like this from the pulpit, try putting it in terms not of the Swedes, like my people, but of the Hittites. They are a long-gone people, and no one will be offended then."

"Good idea!" said the preacher. "That's exactly what I'm going to do."

And sure enough, the next Sunday as he looked out over his congregation from the pulpit, he started, "Okay, there were these two Hittites, Ole and Lena . . ."

Fair enough. Lest any readers be offended, there were these two Hittites, Ole and Sven. They were talking one afternoon, and Ole told Sven, "You know, I tink I'm ready for a little vacation, but dis year I wants to do sumpting a little different. Dees last few years I took your suggestion bout where ta go. Tree years ago you said go ta Hawaii, and Hawaii it was, and Lena, she got pregnant. Da next year you say to go to dem Bahamas, and sure enough, Lena, she gets pregnant again. And last year you tells me Tahiti, and by golly once again Lena comes up pregnant."

Sven asks Ole, "So den what're you gonna do dis year dat's different?"

Ole says, "Dis year I'm gonna take Lena wid me."

Other stories in this rich humor cycle suggest that Sven may not be altogether innocent. One tale has all three characters together at a country-dance, and somewhere between the drinking, dancing, and carousing, Ole loses track of his wife, Lena. He ventures out into the parking area outside the dance hall and checks his car. Sure enough, through the rear window he sees Lena and Sven going at it, making that car rock back and forth like a boat in a storm.

Ole staggers back into the dance hall and announces to everyone with a laugh, "Ho boy! Is dat Sven stinkin' blotto or vat?! He's so drunk, he's out der in my car wit Lena, and he tinks he's *me*!"

When Lena came through Ellis Island upon her arrival in America, an immigration official noted from her papers that she was headed for Wisconsin and weighed in at a hefty 253 pounds. "Well, Lena," the man says. "You are one big girl, all right. Are you going to Wisconsin to play with the Green Bay Packers?"

"Oh no," Lena says indignantly, "I don't play wit no one's but Ole's packer."

Then Ole goes off to war, and on his return, he calls Lena from New York. He wants to warn her that he isn't the man who left her a year before. "Lena, I tink I should tell you dat I vas wounded in dat war, and so when you see me, I will have a purple heart on."

"Oh, dat's okay, Ole. You know I don't care vat color dat ting is just as long as you get it back to me as soon as you can!"

Same Idea, Different Names

It is not a factor that can be accurately quantified, but after more than a half century of hearing and collecting American folk humor, my distinct impression is that in stories with the element of the clueless naïf, the bewildered soul by far and away is most commonly male. Following are a couple of the earliest stories of civil ribaldry that I heard and noted that feature the naive male.

A young lad from Nebraska's Bohemian Alps area once took the family sleigh out on a winter night, picked up his girlfriend, and rode from their hometown of Dodge to a dance over in Howells. Well, it was cold outside, but it was nice and warm under the buffalo robe, and they got to snuggling and smooching as the lights of Howells came into view. So they stopped on a hill and started hugging and kissing a little more seriously, until the young lady breathed huskily, "Lumir . . . I tink I'm ready to go a little further . . ." So he drove her all the way over to Clarkson.

Eric Nielsen told me a similar story that was set near our home in Howard County, Nebraska. This time, however, it was about a Danish lad who was walking his girl from Nysted to a dance at Dannebrog's Pleasure Isle dance hall. Stopping to rest in a barn along the way, the young man thought he'd make his move, but he encountered a problem: he was courting one of the taller girls in the area, and he was having trouble reaching high enough to give her a kiss. Being helpful, the girl suggested that he stand on an anvil that happened to be sitting in the middle of the barn floor. He did and got some fancy kissing done before they moved on.

When they reached another barn along the way, the young man decided that he had enjoyed the first stop so much that some more kissing and hugging was in order, so they went at it again for a while. Then they walked on until they reached the next barn along the route, and there was more of the same. Finally after about the fifth stop, the young man said he had just about all of the loving he could take. The young lady was of course disappointed. She asked if maybe he didn't think she was pretty enough because she was sure willing to continue the fun if he wanted. He admitted that the loving sure was mighty fine and he'd be more than happy to continue, but he just couldn't carry that anvil any farther.

Another young man approaches the father of his girlfriend and asks for her hand in marriage. The father is a little surprised because the boy seems too young to be responsible for his favorite, well-sheltered child. He asks the boy, "How do you intend to support my daughter?"

"Well, sir, she is going to have to support me for the next couple years of school, and when I graduate, I plan to get a job and support her the rest of our lives."

"Son, that's a good plan, but what happens if she gets pregnant during the next two years?"

"I think we'll be all right. We've been lucky so far!"

Exactly the same story told by other narrators ends with quite a different punch line:

"I think we'll be okay. My father told me about the birds and bees, so I figure that if she starts to build a nest, I'll just kick it apart!"

That may have been the same young man who married his high school sweetheart and then didn't show up in town for a couple days, so everyone wondered how his honeymoon had gone. Back at the tavern when he finally did show up, his buddies asked him excitedly, "Hey, did you get her pregnant?"

"I sure hope so," the boy sighed. "I'd hate to go through *that* mess again!"

If tales of civil ribaldry are to be believed, male cluelessness persists right up to and even after the birth of children from a marital union. The new father of a four-pound baby boy complained that he figured he was just lucky "to get his bait back," while another comforted a son whose playmates teased him about being illiterate, "The hell you are! Your ma and me was married six weeks before you was born!"

No Boyz Aloud

A corollary to the oblivious male is the woman who is far more knowledgeable than one expects . . . which I have come to understand in my long life is more a matter of reality than fantasy or fear. Nonetheless, an essential part of humor is surprise, and I suspect that in many rural tales of civil ribaldry what may seem like a surprise to the hapless dupes in the jokes and probably to those who tell and hear the stories is actually a reflection of reality. I once joked about my theory that women go to a common training program called Woman School, where they all learn their crafts and arts to befuddle and frustrate man-kind [*sic*]. A very wise woman indeed then offered to share with me one of the secrets of Woman School—namely, . . . their sacred oath. But she said that she could only let me in on the first five words of that most sacred of secrets. As you can imagine, I held my breath and waited to hear those five words. They are, she told me, "let the man believe that . . ." Again, as is so often the case, the truth far surpasses our wildest imaginings.

A man meets a gorgeous woman in a bar. They talk, they connect, and they end up leaving the party together. They get back to the woman's place, and as she shows him around her apartment, he notices that her bedroom is completely packed with teddy bears. Hundreds of small bears sit on a shelf all the way along the floor, with medium-size ones on a shelf a little higher up the wall and a half-dozen huge teddy bears on the top shelf along the wall.

The man is kind of surprised that this grown and sophisticated woman would have a collection of teddy bears, especially one that's so extensive, but he decides that now is not the time to ask questions. He turns his attention to her. They kiss . . . then they rip each other's clothes off and make mad, passionate love.

After a night of intense passion and as they are lying there together in the afterglow, the man turns to his companion and asks, smiling, "Well, what did you think of *that*?"

The woman says, "You can have any prize from the bottom shelf."

A favorite story of mine since I first began to appreciate joking around follows. I am reminded of a time when I was telling a woman about my book *Everything I Know about Women, I Learned from My Tractor* and I chuckled that I give away so many secrets about men in those pages that I had urged the publisher to splash a banner across the front saying, NOT FOR SALE TO WOMEN WITHOUT WRITTEN PERMISSION FROM AN ADULT MALE! Whereupon Linda muttered half under her breath, "And just where are we supposed to find one of *those*?"

A male friend of mine notes that we all have to grow up, but we don't have to mature. When it comes to jokes about farts, men just never seem to escape adolescence.

A salesman is making his way along a country road through a terrible blizzard when his team is finally stopped in its tracks, and it is obvious that the horses don't intend to go on any farther. Lucky for him, though, through the blowing snow and growing dark he sees a dim lantern glow in a homestead window. He puts the team in a shed by the house and knocks at the door. He is invited into the house, seated by the warm stove, and fed a good meal by the nice-looking widow lady who is the lone occupant of the house.

In their conversation she tells him that the only problem with him staying for the night is that there is only one bed in the tiny sod house, so he'll pretty much have to curl up alongside her under the only blanket she owns. He figures that will be okay, so they get ready for bed. When he crawls under the quilt with her, he asks diplomatically, "Ma'am, I'm just wondering—how do you want me to treat you tonight? As if I were a guest and stranger in your house or would you prefer me to proceed as if I were your husband?"

Well, that widow giggles a little and then says softly, "Since we're here alone and the night is cold and dark, why don't you just go ahead and treat me as if I were your wife?"

So the guy rolls over, farts, and goes to sleep.

Following is a tale I find less and less amusing as I grow older and older:

She was in the kitchen preparing to boil eggs for breakfast. He walked in. She turned and said, "Dear, you have to make love to me right here and now, at this very moment."

As you can imagine, he thought that was quite an offer. His eyes lit up as he thought, "This is my lucky day." And not wanting to lose the moment, he took her into his arms and gave her his very best effort right there on the kitchen table.

Afterward she said, "Thanks," and turned without further comment or reaction to her task at the stove.

More than a little puzzled, he asked, "What was that all about?"

She replied, "My egg timer's broken."

I heard this next story in Dannebrog about the pharmacy that was once here, fifty years ago. And folks are *still* telling the story.

A man had taken some quack medical cure for his, er, male problems (perhaps the same fellow who took the pills that the veterinarian gave the farmer for his slothful bull?), and he found that either he had taken too much of the medication or it was a lot more powerful than advertised. With profound embarrassment and driven only by his continuing discomfort, he went to the village drugstore and found that only the druggist's wife and her sister were behind the counter. At the point of desperation he had no choice but to unbutton his overalls' fly and show them the seriousness of his problem. "Please, ladies, excuse me for asking . . . but what I can get for this?"

After some consultation and whispering, the ladies came back and said, "We've done some figuring, and we're afraid that the best we can do is fifty dollars, as much hard candy as you can get in your pockets, and a ten percent discount on all further purchases this month."

The following is one of my favorite stories of all time and was first told to me as having happened in the Dannebrog Tavern. However, I later heard it told about another tavern in a nearby town, so my guess is that it is widely told and almost certainly widely appreciated. Certainly by me . . .

An aged farmer in overalls sat down at the town tavern's bar next to a primly dressed stranger. "Can I buy you a whiskey?" the old-timer offered by way of hospitality.

"No, thank you," the stranger said. "I tried whiskey once. Didn't like it."

"Well, then, can I offer you a cigar?"

"No, thanks," replied the visitor. "Tried it once. Didn't like it."

"Would you care to join me in a little game of pool then?"

"Thank you, but no. Tried it once. Didn't like it," the fancy fellow said. Then he turned and pointed to a young man at another table and added, "But that's my son over there, and maybe he would like to shoot some pool with you."

"Only child?" the farmer asked.

It's not surprising when children are innocent of the facts of life, or women or rural rubes or old maids. It is less often that grown men almost proudly proclaim a deliberate innocence.

The Church of What?

The careful avoidance of offensive terms in civil ribaldry is not to be confused with prudery; the material is after all *ribald*! And often even a trifle sacrilegious. I think one could rightfully argue, in fact, that much of this type of humor mocks false prudery even while it avoids outright obscenity. Similarly it is my impression that there are nearly as many stories pointing out false piety as there are about other less sensitive ideas. If two people discover they have a common birth date, for instance, the accepted response is, "Our folks must have gone to the same tent meeting!"

Three elders were once bragging about the span of their memories. One said he could remember nursing at his mother's breast. The second said, "That's nothing. I remember the look on my father's face as the midwife delivered me right there in the folks' kitchen." The third gent won the contest, however, when he declared, "I remember going to a revival meeting with Dad and coming home with Mom."

A common expression here is, "Never go fishing with just one Baptist because he'll drink all your beer." It is merely an extension of another common commentary: "Jews don't recognize Christ, Lutherans don't recognize the pope, and Baptists don't recognize each other in a liquor store."

Or why don't Baptists have sex while standing up? Because it might lead to dancing.

A story persists about a community picnic one summer

when some young rascals decided to improve the fun by plugging the watermelons cooling on ice in the stock tank and lacing each of them with a pint of moonshine. Later the Lutheran minister was seen eating watermelon as fast as he could stuff it into his mouth. The Catholic priest allegedly stashed six of them under a blanket in his buggy. And the Baptist minister filled his pockets with seeds.

A story told as fact was said to have happened near Dannebrog at the bridge across the Loup River, which runs just below the window where I am writing these words. As was (and still is!) common on hot summer days, a local gent decided to cool down and go skinny-dipping in the river. He went down along the bank and around the curve just west of here. He left his clothing in a pile behind a cedar bush near the bridge but kept his straw hat on to avoid getting his face and nose sunburned. He made his way upstream and then lay back in the cool, clean water, letting the current drift him back downstream toward the bridge—a practice we still enjoy in the same river and refer to it as "butt bouncing." But as this gentleman approached the bridge, he heard voices, so he pulled himself toward the shore and peeked through the shrubs to find—oh no!—the preacher's wife was hosting the church's annual picnic for the ladies' auxiliary on the bank near the bridge. That is, between him and his cached clothing. He lowered himself back into the water and quietly mulled over his options: he could cover his private parts with his hat to preserve his *dignity*, make a mad dash through the gathering, grab his clothes, and head for cover up the bank; or he could cover his face with his hat to preserve his *identity* and make the same run. He decided on the latter. So holding the hat over his face, he dashed among the startled and screaming women, grabbed his clothes, and hotfooted it through the trees toward town.

Once they had recovered from their astonishment and regained their voices, one woman decided to defend her family's honor. She said, "I can tell you one thing—that was *not* my husband."

Whereupon a second woman insisted, "Well, it wasn't anybody from my family."

But the conversation came to a stop when the preacher's wife said, "I'm pretty sure it was no one from *this* congregation."

A preacher was outraged one day to find that his bicycle had been stolen and, asking around the town, was not able to find any clues to its whereabouts. So he decided that he would confront his congregation from the pulpit in hopes of uncovering the thief. He based his sermon that Sunday on the Ten Commandments, planning to stop dramatically, pause, and survey the congregants for a guilty reaction when he reached the eighth one, the prohibition against stealing. He went through the first of God's laws quickly, getting nods from his parishioners when he reminded them not to worship other gods, make graven images, or take the Lord's name in vain. He got some "amens" with keeping the Sabbath and honoring one's mother and father. There were scattered "hosannas" and "hallelujahs" with the prohibition on killing. But then he amazed everyone when he ended the sermon abruptly and dismissed his flock with a quick final prayer. As they filed out the church door and into the village street, one of the church elders stopped and asked why the preacher had so abruptly ended his sermon before finishing the recitation of the Decalogue.

The preacher muttered with chagrin, "When I got to the seventh commandment, I remembered where I left my bicycle."

For all I know, that story may well be only the conclusion to this next one. You can gauge the antiquity of this story by the ancient notion of a doctor making house calls.

A young doctor moved to a country village to replace a doctor who was retiring. The older doctor suggested that the youngster accompany him on his rounds so the community could get to know him and he could get to know the community. At the first house the woman complained that she'd been sick to her stomach. The veteran doctor says, "You've probably been overdoing it with the fresh fruit. Why don't you cut back a bit on what you've been eating and see if that doesn't take care of the problem."

As they left, the young man said, "You didn't examine that woman at all closely. How did you arrive at your diagnosis?"

"Well, when I dropped my stethoscope on the floor and bent down to pick it up, I noticed a half-dozen banana peels in the wastebasket. That was probably what was making her sick."

The younger doctor was impressed and said, "That's very clever. If you don't mind, I think I'd like to try that kind of observation at our next stop."

At the next house the doctors spent a little time talking with the young woman, who complained that she had been feeling very run down and tired lately. The young doctor thought about the problem a moment and then said, "You've probably been doing too much volunteer work for the church. Maybe you should cut back on your devotions, and perhaps that will help you get more rest."

As they left, the older doctor said, "I know that woman well. Your diagnosis is probably correct. She's very active in the church, but how did you figure that out so quickly?"

The newcomer said, "I did what you did at that last stop. And when I dropped my stethoscope and bent down to pick it up, I saw the pastor hiding under the bed."

The motif of the experienced veteran instructing the young apprentice is not unusual in any humor, rural or urban. A common story from my youth told of the elderly priest counseling the young replacement for him at the parish and reassuring him after a crushing reaction to his first Mass, "You did fine, my son. The only problem was that the correct announcement for upcoming activities was supposed to be for a 'taffy pull at St. Peter's.'"

Cross-sectarian stories are particularly typical. They're as common as the usually (but not always!) friendly competition between congregations in any small town.

Three guys are in a really serious situation and fear that their demise is imminent. "Friends," one says, "What we really need to do here . . . in fact, the only hope we have left . . . is to pray." The other two say they have no idea where to start. They haven't been to church in decades, have little faith in God, and certainly haven't faced any occasion this dire that called for prayer.

The first one finally says, "Well, I happen to live right across the road from a Catholic church, so I have overheard enough over the years that maybe I can rise to this occasion. Bow your heads, and let us pray: B12 . . . N16 . . . O8 . . ."

Some stories touching on the church and community are simply funny, with no moral content at all. Maybe.

An elderly couple here in my own village were once sitting on their front porch swing on a pleasant summer evening, listening to the cicadas singing in the trees and the Lutheran church choir practicing down the street. Speaking of the choir and its hymns, the wife said, "That must be just about the most pleasant sound in the world."

To her astonishment, however, her husband misunderstood and responded, "I understand that they make that sound by rubbing their legs together."

What Did He Say?

Carriers of tales in the genre of civil ribaldry are mostly male in my experience, which is perhaps a result of the fact that I am male and so are most of my friends. Inheritance of the art seems to be a factor. As you have read in earlier pages of this collection, one of the finest storytellers in our village is Eric, son of Bumps Nielsen, a master of the craft. However, Bumps's wife and Eric's mother, Harriett, is famous for being as unskilled in the humorous narrative as Eric, like his late dad, is a classical master.

Whenever Eric starts a story, a crowd gathers to admire the performance, and in a way that is also true of Harriett. Nothing is funnier in our town than Harriett's screwing up one of her stories. She draws a crowd when she begins to tell a story because everyone in town understands there will be hilarity . . . and a good laugh (including from Harriett herself) when she forgets the punch line of her story, drops it too early in the story, or completely garbles it. For example, a classic from Harriett's repertoire is one of her own favorites. As it was told to her originally, two farmers from this area go to the city and find themselves at a stoplight beside a car full of smart-alecky city high school boys. One of the kids drops his pants and slams his rear against the window of the car he is in, mooning the farmers. "What do we do now, Frank?" asks one farmer, and the other says, "Show 'em your nuts, Fred." Thereupon Fred puts his thumbs in his ears, waggles his fingers, crosses his eyes, sticks out his tongue, and yells, "Nyah nyah nyah nyah!"

Harriett liked that story so much that after hearing it the first time, she charged to the Dannebrog Tavern to tell it to the crowd at the tavern's Big Table. She got through the story just fine until she got to Frank's line, which she misphrased as "show 'em your balls," whereupon she went through the motions the first joke teller had used. What was hilarious to Harriett's audience was that the punch line is obvious enough that they could deduce what she *should* have said, but the resulting humor was even funnier because of what Harriett so incongruously did in fact say.

Curiously and beyond my ability to explain is a phenomenon known locally as "Harriett's story," a narrative that has become exclusively hers, perhaps because to everyone's amazement she tells it again and again with perfect timing and without error. Mirable dictu. Our village is very small, and anything that happens on the main street can be seen and heard by just about anyone. So the moment we hear a woman's voice shouting, "WHAT DID HE SAY?" we all chuckle, because we all know that Harriett has found an occasion and a new audience for *her* story. And here for your enjoyment (minus only the pleasure of hearing Harriett tell it) *is* Harriett's story:

A young man is driving south down Iowa's Interstate 29 and stops somewhere north of Council Bluffs to get a cup of coffee and a piece of pie. He winds up seated at the lunch counter next to an elderly couple and strikes up a friendly conversation. "Where are you folks from?"

"We're from up in Sioux City," the old gent says.

The old lady yells, "WHAT DID HE SAY?" And her husband shouts back into her ear, "HE WANTS TO KNOW WHERE WE'RE FROM, AND I TOLD HIM WE'RE FROM SIOUX CITY!"

"And where are you two headed then?" the young man asks. And the old man says, "Oh, we're going down south to Kansas City."

Then the old lady yells, "WHAT DID HE SAY?" And her husband shouts into her ear, "HE WANTS TO KNOW WHERE WE'RE GOING, AND I TOLD HIM WE'RE HEADED TO KANSAS CITY!"

The young man says, "You know, the worst sex I ever had in my life was in Kansas City."

The old lady yells, "WHAT DID HE SAY?"

The old man yells into her ear, "HE SAYS HE KNOWS YOUR SISTER!"

While these stories, folklore in general and humor in particular, reveal a good deal about the culture in which they arise and thrive, they also say plenty about the person who has remembered the story and added it to his or her own recitative inventory. We tend to laugh about those things that concern us, bother us, and even frighten or distress us—that is, about our own foibles and weaknesses. There was a time when I spoke of this tendency to my university folklore students, and then I told them my two favorite stories. As the modern phrase has it, it occurred to me at some point that I was probably oversharing—that is, saying far more about myself than I wanted to.

The tale of civil ribaldry is not a naked gag line but a story. If there is a punch line, it may be so subtle that it takes real thought and imagination to grasp the humor of that narrative. And whatever prurience is perceived and perhaps objected to is only in the ear of the hearer. In fact, it depends on the *understanding* of the listener. Here is an example of this kind of evocative humor without a narrative structure, nonetheless exhibiting and eliciting imagery only in the mind of the prurient audience:

How can you spot a show-off in a nudist colony? He's

the one carrying two cups of hot coffee and a half-dozen doughnuts at the same time.

I wish there were some way to probe the minds of those who most enjoy these jokes, those who understand them instantly, those who only slowly or never figure out what the point of the jokes is, and those who find them worthy enough to pass along the line of tradition. Me, for example. Here's a longer example with a clear plot line:

A farmer drives into a neighbor's yard and knocks at the door. One of the family's boys comes out and greets the visitor.

> VISITOR: Is your pa home?
>
> BOY: No, sir, he ain't. He went to town.
>
> VISITOR: Well, then, is your ma here?
>
> BOY: No, sir, she ain't here neither. She went into town with Pa.
>
> VISITOR: How about your brother, Lester? Is he here?
>
> BOY: Nope. He's with Ma and Pa. Is there anything I can do for you?
>
> VISITOR: Nah, I don't believe so. I really wanted to talk to your pa about your brother, Lester, getting my oldest daughter pregnant.
>
> BOY [*after thinking about the issue a minute*]: You'll have to talk to Pa about that. I know that Pa charges fifty dollars for the bull and twenty-five for the boar, but I really don't know what he gets for Lester.

The story may be brief, but there is dialogue and a plot and, as the maxim goes, a beginning, a middle, and an ending. In another example:

A woman goes into a bar and sees a cowboy with his feet propped up on the table, and he has the biggest feet she has ever seen. She gets to thinking and asks the cowboy if it's true what they say about men with big feet. The cowboy says, "It sure is. Come with me over to my place, and I'll show you." She thinks that sounds just fine, so she goes with him and spends the night at his place.

The next morning as she leaves, she hands the cowboy a hundred-dollar bill. A little embarrassed and confused, he stammers, "I'm really flattered, sweetheart. Nobody has ever paid me before for the favor."

The woman turns on her heels and heads out the door, saying, "The money is not for the 'favor.' Take it and buy yourself some boots that fit!"

How You Gonna Keep 'Em Down on the Farm (after They've Seen the Farm)?

With thanks to Abe Burroughs via Dick Cavett

I hope not to be demeaning (although I suppose I am) in saying that I believe the subtlety of these rural tales reflects a certain sophistication on the part of the tellers and their audiences as opposed therefore to a lack of it in modern, more urban folklore (understanding that it has become urbanized not simply by its content or context but also through the fact that the Plains and America are increasingly more urban rather than rural). Today we get our entertainment from television, YouTube, Twitter, email forwards, or any other form of "social media." Now our patience is short, and our willingness to devote intellectual tools that appeal to our sense of humor has therefore suffered. In places where time moves slower—at card games in small-town cafés, with small groups of men leaning over pickup truck hoods or on a fence gate while admiring a herd of beef cattle, over lunch in a rural tavern—subtlety is still the coin of the realm.

Otherwise, I must note, like the modern legend, folklore may indeed find a more hospitable home in the cities because one now finds a lack of sophistication and intellectual curiosity there. Obviously that was not always the case. At one time a folklorist could presume that the farmer-peasant's knowledge and culture were necessarily steeped in folklore because transmission through unsophisticated means was the standard, whereas smarty-pants methods such as printed matter, lectures, concerts, university classrooms, or gallery displays were citified stuff. Now it is the other way around: farming is a highly technological, sophisticated system while urban-industrial living is not.

The format of folklife may not be as elaborate or as technical as high culture, but the content and audience reception may nonetheless be much the same. Some years ago an educated, highly ranked woman in the state government told me she had been visiting a small town in north-central Nebraska when, due to unforeseen circumstances, she found herself in the town over a Saturday night. She asked the man at the desk of the five-unit motel where she was staying what there might be to do in a small Nebraska town on a Saturday night. "Not much," he said. "You know, there's the tavern . . . Drinking with the cowboys, playing pool. That's about it, what with there not being a wedding or anything like that going on this weekend."

She expressed her disappointment and said she really wanted to see what life was like in the small town and to do what the local folks do. After a pause, and perhaps detecting that my friend was a sophisticated city girl and therefore ready for pretty much anything, he added, hesitantly, "Well, there are the old boys who meet over at the Co-op."

The "old boys?" Who "meet over at the Co-op?" Well, that did it for Mary Ethel. She pushed for further information as she had to know more about this cultural event, which sounded almost seductively subversive. And finally the old gent reluctantly directed her to the Co-op's supplies barn over where the grain elevators stood at the edge of the town. He told her to knock at the big door to the seed-and-feed shed, to explain at the door that he had sent her, and to brace herself for some fancy, big city–style entertainment.

Now, I think most people—maybe even I—would say, "Thanks, that's all right. Think I'll just sit in my motel room and watch something on the television." But not Mary Ethel. (She has now gone on to a wilder party in the sky, so I know for a fact [1] that she wouldn't mind my revealing at least her given names and [2] that everyone who knew Mary Ethel will *instantly* recognize her.) She went to the Co-op, knocked at the door, and assured the old gent opening the door that she was there for what he was there for, that she was ready for anything, and that whatever happened in Centralia would stay in Centralia. (I am falsifying that name to protect any old geezers whose wives think they are in town for a prayer meeting.)

What she found was one of the joys of her anecdotal life. And I envied her the experience. It seems that a clutch of local geezers gathered once a month or so at the darkened, windowless Co-op, having booked for their entertainment one of the many third-level exotic dancers who circulate (I understand) from one small-town tavern to the next. They sat on seed and chicken feed sacks to watch her dance to whatever she happened to bring along on her portable boom box and . . . this detail is what, I am embarrassed to admit, speaks most to my prurient imagination . . . illuminating the stripper's moves—I have to stop to laugh!—with their flashlights! Again in my deviant fantasies, I imagine those panting old gents focusing their beams (as it were) on those parts of the dancer's anatomy that most recharged their aging but still vital batteries.

Alexander Payne, the director of *Nebraska*, *must* put that scene into a movie somewhere along the line.

The point cannot be overstated (even if my preceding example is over the line): where humor is indeed rural in nature, content, context, and transmission, the humor can be so subtle that it takes an agile mind to recognize it. Okay, watching a stripper dance while one is seated on a feed sack in a darkened co-op barn and spotlighting her delectables with a flashlight might not be what most people would call subtle, but you have to admit it requires some imagination.

For a less prurient and subtler story—I was once in a circle of academics comprising some economists, some agricultural scientists, and one farmer-rancher. One of the highly educated and theoretical scholars asked the farmer how his corn had done that year in his county, and he replied, "Not as good as expected, but then no one thought it would be." The conversation continued among the academics without so much as a hiccup of hesitation, and I imagine I might not have paused or changed my level of thought had the farmer not winked in my direction and broken into a sly smile. To this day I can repeat that conversation and punch line in many circles without a single person, no matter how educated or urbane, detecting the logical flaw, leaving me to try to explain it, sometimes simply by repeating the line with emphasis to make the oxymoron clear.

It's not as if the rural denizen fails to understand that there is a difference, or what the differences are, between urban and rural life. When my friend Eric took over management of the village tavern, he told me that he had been to Omaha and, thinking to elevate the tone of his new establishment, visited some bistros in the Paris of the Pig Belt. He told me that he noted with interest that many of the city's evening spots served hors d'oeuvres at no charge before meals, or they at least offered snacks, always salty, to encourage the purchase of drinks, where the real profit of such an establishment lies. So he was thinking of just placing a livestock salt block on each table at the tavern so people coming in for a meal would lick the block, get thirsty, and increase his beer sales.

Moreover, he had gone to another eatery where patrons went in the door and could select either a steak from a large glass-fronted cooler or a lobster from a huge display aquarium for their dining pleasure. Eric, knowing full well the epicurean taste of *his* clientele, was thinking of having a special Rocky Mountain Oyster Friday when he would run a flock of sheep through the tavern so diners could pick precisely which ones would be the source of *their* evening meal.

In another conversation Eric considered a dress code for his establishment. I suggested that he might require not just a coat and tie but even recommend ascots. A rural friend who was also at the table asked, "What the hell is an ascot?"

Eric, with obvious indignation, said, "Well, you dumb shit, that's French for 'snail'!"

Jim Harrison, novelist, epicure, bon vivant, and friend, was once in town with me and noted that a large service station and repair garage directly on the main intersection of our village was for sale. We strolled over there and looked in the windows before heading to the tavern for lunch. Jim said, "You know, Rog, we should buy this building. Here in the old tire repair bay we could put an old tractor or two and have a complete set of the finest tools you can buy—Snap-ons, maybe. And here in the middle, where the office and reception area were, we could have the kitchen. Over here, in the service bay, we would put the most comfortable furniture we could find . . . maybe something European and antique."

As Jim considered his plans for the abandoned filling station, he paused, rubbed his chin, and peered again into the building's interior. He wasn't so much talking to me as he was expressing thoughts as they passed through his mind.

"This would be an establishment with prix fixe. We'd come in at the appointed time and be greeted by a gorgeous, young, naked woman who would pour us the very best martinis conceivable. We would sit, relax, talk, and drink. After some time—plenty of time—another beautiful, young, naked woman would come in, open and pour a bottle of the very best wine, and present a salad . . . fresh, crisp, with superb handmade dressing. And we would nibble and sip while again enjoying erudite conversation.

"Another beautiful, young, naked woman would come in

the room, ring a small silver bell, and we would adjourn to the tractor bay, where we would select the very best torque wrench or breaker bar or ridge reamer, and delight ourselves a quarter hour or so while working on the tractor. Then another beautiful, young, naked woman would come in, ring a small silver bell, and we would repair again to the dining bay, where the most superb entrée ever imagined is already on the table, ready for our appreciation.

"And so it would go, Rog. Course after course. All the while attended by the most beautiful, fully naked women we could find. (It's clothing that carries germs, you know.) Until at the very end, there'd be the best port, the finest Stilton and imported English walnuts, the best Bosc pears for the perfect dessert."

Jim leaned back on his heels, immersed and delighted with his fantasy. But then he leaned forward, looked me in the eye with his one good eye, and said with some seriousness, "But you know, Rog . . . if we were to start something like that, sure as hell . . . they'd make us open it to the public."

Birds Do It, Bees Do It

With the context for so many of these stories being rural and agricultural, I suppose it's not surprising that bestiality, from the gentle and mild to the truly gross, becomes a topic and that sometimes the animals are presented as the initiators of the interaction. There is sex, and then there is, well, uh . . . sex. Bumps Nielsen, the richest repository for such stories in this area and now sadly gone, left me with plenty of examples.

As a traveling salesman approached Widow Jensen's house, her vicious dog came tearing around the corner and chased him up a sycamore tree. The widow came out her door and yelled up to the salesman, "Don't worry about the dog. I had him castrated."

"Ma'am," the drummer yelled back, maintaining a safe altitude, "I don't think that's what he had in mind."

Also from Bumps is another story along the same lines but actually a 180-degree reversal:

An old coot was visiting a widow lady when her lap dog strolled over and lifted his leg on the old gent. The man jumped up, the lady apologized, and the man, severely embarrassed by the situation, said, "That's okay. I was afraid he was about to kick me."

For personal reasons I find it perfectly reasonable that there seems to be less rural humor about cats. I first heard this next one during a conversation at the Dannebrog Tavern's Big Table.

Old farmer Harris had a constipated cat. Seems it was plugged up with a hairball. The day he called the veterinarian, Harris had misplaced his false teeth so his speech was not good. The vet was out on a call, so Harris told the vet's assistant the problem he had, and the assistant thought he'd said "calf" instead of "cat." So the assistant suggested that administering a quart of mineral oil might take care of the problem.

When the vet came in, the assistant told him what he had done. The vet knew Harris didn't have a calf on the place, so he called the old farmer to see what he actually might have wanted. Realizing Harris was really asking about a cat, the vet said, "You didn't give that cat a quart of mineral oil, did you?"

"Sure did," Harris said.

"Where's that cat now?" asked the vet.

"Out in the yard with five other cats," the farmer replied.

"What are they doing?" the vet wanted to know.

Harris said, "Two's diggin', two's coverin', and one's huntin' new ground."

A common example of civil ribaldry that I have heard here over the years is about the young man who comes back to the farm after his military service and wonders if all the critters on the farm remember him after his long absence. As he walks up to the house, his old dog, Shep, comes running out of the house with his tail wagging. The man goes out to the barn, where Bessie the cow immediately recognizes him and moos her welcome. Then he ventures out to the pasture, where all the sheep back up to a stump.

One of the first examples of civil ribaldry I ran upon in my early collecting is also the one with the most startling imagery.

A bunch of guys were talking about the first time they had had sex. One had a screamer. The second had a biter. But one big lug was just hanging back and not saying a word.

Finally the others started ribbing him about his silence and tried to get him to tell about his first experience. So finally he kicked the dust with his boot toes and stammered, "I'll tell you, boys, it was plenty rough all right." Whereupon he pulled off his shirt and turned around, revealing a back covered with deep and livid scars.

"Holy cow!" one of his friends gasped. "So she was a scratcher then? Did she do that with her fingernails?"

"Nah," the clodhopper chuckled. "That's what happened when the single tree broke and the running gear passed over me."

You have to be a veteran farm boy to understand *that* one!

An example I heard early in my interest in civil ribaldry featured a farmer who was accused by an outraged neighbor of sodomizing one of his cows. When the neighbor took him to court, the judge instructed the litigant, "Describe exactly what happened."

"Well, Judge," he said sternly, "I woke up in the middle of the night and looked out the bedroom window, and there was Ferd pulling a wood crate up behind ol' Bessie. He got all set just right, dropped the straps of his overalls, raised up Bessie's tail, and was just about ready to get to business when that cow cut loose and blew fresh manure all over him."

The judge was about to bang his gavel and declare Ferd guilty when one of the jurors whispered loudly, "They'll do it every time!"

The judge dismissed the case.

Indiscreet Secretions

A topic certainly worthy of civil ribaldry is excrement . . . an undainty subject to be dealt with delicately. Well, ... sort of delicately anyway.

One day Lyle was at the café's card table when the conversation turned somehow to bears. He told us that when he was stationed in Alaska during the Korean War, everyone in the camp was constantly on the lookout for bears marauding garbage cans. A trip to the latrine at night under those conditions could result in a life-and-death confrontation. The men were instructed, he said, that if they were ever faced with a belligerent bear and had to resort to emergency measures, they should stuff a handful of human excrement into the bear's nose because it is a very effective repellant for any kind of bear, including grizzly and polar bears.

Of course, someone at the table asked, understandably, "In a situation like that, where the heck are you supposed to come up with a handful of human excrement?"

Without even looking up from his hand of cards, Lyle replied, "Just reach around behind you. It'll be there!"

A popular story appearing in many variations in this region since the late 1990s tells about an elderly gentleman getting his annual physical checkup. He's finishing up when the doctor tells him that before he goes, he should leave urine, stool, and semen samples. Along with all the other usual afflictions and humiliations of aging (I write this from increasing personal experience, I should note), this man was also deaf, so he turns to his wife (oh, this is so familiar!) and asks her, "WHAT DID HE SAY?"

The old lady says to him with some disgust, "He wants you to leave your underwear."

Why Is It Called a "Fly?"

Embarrassing but less disgusting, even if more public, is the male faux pas of the unclosed fly. I have been in a circle of locals occasionally when one of our friends has come along with "his barn door open," as the phrase goes, so I have had the good fortune to hear the standard remarks and the guys' innovative responses.

"Hey, Ralph, your hood is open. And it looks like the engine has gone south on you there."

"Are you airing that thing out again, Ralph?"

"Or are you advertising?"

"I think he's getting a head start on his next trip to the men's room."

Ralph showed himself to be up to the moment, however, when he replied, "Nope, by golly, I missed a chance thirty years ago, and I'm not about to let it happen again."

At some point, I should have warned my friend, it might be best to keep secrets secret. I heard one about a fellow who walks into the grocery store, and the pretty young girl behind the checkout points at his pants fly and says, "Mr. Smith, did you know your barracks door is open?"

Figuring he missed a chance thirty years ago and wasn't going to let it happen again, Mr. Smith asked lasciviously, "Can you see inside that barracks door, Heather?"

"Why, yes, I can," the young girl giggled.

"And do you see an able-bodied soldier standing at attention?"

Heather looked a bit more closely and then said sweetly, "Noooo, all I see in there is a disabled veteran taking a nap on a couple of old duffel bags."

As noted earlier, the best way to disarm insults among friends at the tavern, around the café's card table, or thrown between pickup trucks idling on Main Street is to laugh at them and then turn them aside with an equally clever and more-often-than-not self-deprecating remark of one's own. Russell is frequently ribbed about his ample girth, and he effectively defuses the comments by noting that "when you have a valuable piece of equipment, you should always put a shed over it." On another occasion an equally full-figured friend answered an insult about his girth with this comment: "There are still plenty of women who like to work in the shade."

A curiosity, I find, to those not familiar with male sociology is the role of the insult among friends. Conversations between male friends—good, close friends, that is!—are freckled all over with small insults. In fact, sometimes entire conversations among a circle of friends are little other than insults. The prevalence, acceptance, and even importance of mutual, good-natured insulting in male circles became dramatically apparent to me some years ago when I noticed that whenever a man who was generally despised in our very small community came into the tavern while a lively, happy exchange of stories, anecdotes, comments, and, yes, insults was in full swing, the place would suddenly fall silent. When other men came in, they were greeted often as not by insults about the disarray of their clothing, the cut of their hair, the disrepair of their pickup truck, and their late arrival or that they arrived at all. Then they were invited to join the table, with the first round having been already ordered and paid for. But when Charlie walked in, there was no greeting, no comment, and most definitely no insults. No one liked Charlie enough to insult him. Oh, he freely insulted others but without any hint of cheer. It was clear to me: Charlie was not liked well enough to insult.

Geriatric Indignities

Not surprising, almost certainly the most common subject of civil ribaldry within any circle of elders, and the stories I hear more and more often and appreciate less and less as I grow older, are those of waning virility. In fact in a small town not far from here—and I assure you, this *is* a true story even though I will protect the dignity and reputation of the community by not revealing its name—an old storefront converted to a social building where men can play cards, drink coffee, and tell lies is known by everyone, including the ladies of the village, as "The Dead Pecker Club." A common excuse for the declared inadequacy is, "All that saltpeter they fed me in the army is finally taking effect."

Understandably, there is considerable overlap between tales about old age and impotence and those about September-May marriages. Or November-Sometime-after-Thanksgiving and Springtime-before-Even-the-Dandelions-Bloom relationships. I offer the following story by way of example.

An eighty-five-year-old man marries a lovely twenty-five-year-old woman. Because her new husband is so old, the woman decides that on their wedding night they should have separate hotel suites. She is concerned that the old fellow might do himself some damage if there isn't a wall and door between them at least that first night. After the wedding festivities, she prepares herself for bed and for the knock she expects at her door.

Sure enough the knock comes, and there is her groom, ready for action. They unite in conjugal union and all goes well, whereupon he takes his leave of her and she prepares to go to sleep for the night. After a few minutes there's a knock on the door, and there the old guy is again, ready for more action. Somewhat surprised she consents, and again they are successful, after which the old-timer bids her good night and leaves.

She is certainly ready for some sleep at this point and is just nodding off when she hears another knock at the door, and there he is again, fresh as a twenty-five-year-old and ready for more. Once again the couple goes at it. They are enjoying the afterglow when the young bride says to him, "I am really impressed that a guy your age has enough, uh, energy to go for it three times. I've been with guys less than half your age who were only good for one time."

Puzzled, the old gent turns to her and asks, "I was already here?"

The classic line about male aging is, "The mind is the second thing to go." Many of the tales of civil ribaldry that men tell refer precisely to those first two losses.

A local citizen walking by Kerry's Grocery one day sees an old-timer sitting on a park bench, sobbing his heart out. So the compassionate gentleman sits down beside the old fellow and tries to comfort him, asking if there's anything he can do to help. The old man just shakes his head and keeps on sobbing. "Why don't you just talk with me about it, and maybe I can help," the Good Samaritan says. "Now, come on. What's the problem?"

The old guy catches his breath and sobs out his story: "About a year ago I married this beautiful, wealthy young woman a good fifty years younger than I am. Every night she gives me a bath, rubs me down, puts scented oils on me, dresses me in silk pajamas, takes me to our huge round bed, and makes love to me. In the morning I wake up to the smell of coffee and bacon and eggs cooking. She goes off to her work in town but then rushes home to fix me a nice lunch—a steak sandwich maybe or a big slab of meat loaf. When she comes home in the evening, she scrambles to bring me a couple of cold beers and immediately gets busy cooking a big supper while I read the evening papers. Then it's time for a bath, massage, bed, and exquisite love-making again." And with that the old man falls into further spasms of sobbing.

"That all sounds pretty good to me," says the man who is trying to comfort him. "Where the heck is the problem in all that?"

"I can't," the old man sobs, "I can't . . . I can't remember where I live!"

Just as my perspective on the nature of the forms I am calling civil ribaldry may be skewed by the facts that I do live in the rural countryside (one is not likely to find stories about outhouses in urban Omaha) and that that countryside sits in the middle of America (stories that feature a cornfield would not be as common in New Hampshire), I am sure other factors mean that I hear some stories more often than other ones and do not hear other tales at all: I am male, I am—it hurts to admit it—elderly, and thirty-five years ago I married my Lovely Linda, a woman eighteen years younger than I am. I will have to leave it to other collectors and researchers of traditional lore to determine to what degree those factors have skewed the body of material I have recorded for my own files these last fifty years. For the time being, however, I can only work with the stories I have, and they tend to be male oriented, to deal with male aging, and to concentrate perhaps atypically on the situation of the old man with the young bride.

Even when I was a young man myself, I heard and was amused by tales and laments eulogizing lost male vigor. I was only seventeen, for example, when I first heard a poem recited by my one-time father-in-law Oscar Henry and was struck even then by what I would later label its "civil ribaldry":

> Those olden days I oft remember,
> Those youthful days of joy and fun,
> When all my joints were lithe and limber.
> Did I say all? Yes, all but one.
>
> Now I'm getting daily older,
> Those youthful days of joy have gone;
> My joints are getting daily stiffer,
> Did I say all? Yes, all but one.

Linda and I married in 1981, and about six months beforehand I started hearing a sudden explosion of stories about old men associating with younger women. Funny how that happens. There were the usual repeats of the canard about the elderly gent who was warned that bedtime activities with a vigorous young woman can be dangerous to one's health, to which he replies notoriously, "If she dies, she dies."

We had only just begun our relationship when Linda introduced me to her best friend. The woman looked us over (Linda was then twenty-six) and asked with obvious unease, "Uh, Linda, when are you going to introduce him to your parents?"

And Linda quipped, "Right after the first baby."

I've been reminded again and again of the old preacher who took a young wife and was cautioned by his vicar that she would more likely than not be expecting "more than a laying on of hands." One wonders how far removed from the truth some of the traditional stories about such arrangements are.

An old man marries a young woman, and one night not long into their marriage he manages what he considers to be an almost heroic performance in bed. To his surprise, his bride just sighs and rolls over to go to sleep. "Is that all you have to say?" he asks in disappointment.

"What do you mean?" she asks.

"What happened to all the moaning, groaning, screaming, and howling?"

"Oh," she explained, "I save that for when I am faking it."

Not far removed from that tale is again the common narrative about the young bride who was sobbing mightily at the door as she waved good-bye to her old farmer husband as he was setting off with a load of produce and going to the city for a couple days. The old gent, thinking he would comfort her, went quietly to embrace her and whispered in her ear, "There, there, dear. You'll be all right. Just keep in mind how we made love last night."

She looked up with her big blue eyes and said, "Why do you think I'm crying?"

I was also told about the old man with the young bride who appealed to his doctor because a year had passed since the nuptials and there was still no baby. The doctor suggested that at his age it was doubtful that a child would ever be in the picture and that if he really wanted that progeny he just might have to bring a hired hand over to his farm for the job. A couple months later the doctor met the old gent on the streets of town. The doc asked him if he had taken on that hired hand as recommended and how things were going. "Just fine," the old man beamed. "The wife is pregnant. And so is the hired girl!"

An old man is having trouble keeping up, if you catch my drift, with his young wife and consults with his doctor. Or maybe it was the bartender down at the town tavern. Doesn't matter. In the country it's pretty much the same thing. The adviser recommends that the old gent buy a dozen oysters and see if maybe eating them might not pick things up, as it were. Later the old fellow comes back to his counselor with a long, sad face, explaining, "Only six of them oysters worked!" (I should note that in the spirit of having reported that these tales are predominantly rural in nature, I have heard this same story with a dozen eggs rather than oysters.)

I can imagine the reference to oysters might be puzzling to some. There was a time when oysters were to a man in need, as it were, as Cialis and Viagra are for such gents today. Although for all you might guess from the television advertisements, the primary improvement those drugs provide is to enable a man to throw a football through a tire swing or to help with fancy moves during dance lessons. (Linda says the couples pictured in those advertisements for what are colloquially known as "wick stiffeners" are obviously not married because they keep smiling at each other.)

So for the purpose of these old-time stories, let it be stipulated that oysters have long been considered what they call on television "a male enhancement." Camp commanders of frontier forts often established a precise distance at which "hog farms," or cribs for prostitutes, had to be removed from the military grounds, so of course that is *precisely* where they were built, to the foot distance. If upon finding building ruins with multiple small stalls there is any question whether they are indeed the soldiers' "relief stations," all the field archeologist has to do to verify the find is to dig in the refuse piles behind the buildings or, if really lucky, in the location of an old outhouse. If oyster cans sliced open with a knife or field bayonet in a cross pattern are found . . . Eureka! The thing is, if a soldier was going to travel through the bleak and sometimes dangerous frontier landscape to find some comfort in the arms of a woman, he had hopes, as he did in his armaments, of going into the fray with a repeater rather than a single-shot breechloader. So to speak.

An old-timer marries a beautiful young woman many, *many* years his junior, and very early in the marriage they have exactly the problems one might expect. The woman tries to explain her frustration to the old gent, but with her sense of propriety (and in the spirit of civil ribaldry, I might add!), she can't bring herself to tell him explicitly what she feels is missing in the relationship. They finally go to a marriage counselor, who can see just from looking at the couple where the difficulties might lie, and the more he looks at the young lady and imagines her unmet needs, the more eager he is to . . . well, help the couple get through their problems. So finally he says, "I realize that neither of you wants to talk about this issue in graphic detail, so I'll spare you that embarrassment. Let me illustrate how you can get things back on track in your marriage." The marriage counselor leads the beautiful young woman over to his office couch, undresses her with obvious relish, embraces her, caresses her, passionately plants kisses all over her entire body, and concludes with activities of his wildest fantasies and in a variety of positions. Only occasionally dozing off, the old husband watches it all with some interest and even now and then amazement.

Finally when both the adviser and the young woman were utterly exhausted, the counselor retreated to his desk. Then he gasped, "That's what your wife needs. And I mean at least three times a week. Do you think you can do it?"

The old man thought about it a couple minutes and then said, "Well, I can drop her off here on Mondays and Wednesdays, but Fridays are my days to go fishing."

A different take on the scenario tells of two men who are commiserating in the town tavern one morning, with one suffering from a horrendous hangover from the previous night's excesses. "Tell you what I do for hangovers," the buddy says. "I get my wife to come back to bed after we wake up, and we go to it. That takes my mind off my problems and sets me up feeling just fine for the rest of the day.

I'm telling you, that really takes care of a hangover. You should try it."

His suffering friend says, "By golly, that *does* sound like a good idea. Do you think your wife is at home?"

If you believe what you see on television, "erectile dysfunction" is the primary health problem in America today, but as noted previously, the prescribed medications appear not to do much more than make men want to dance. There are examples, however, of the stuff working.

An old-timer goes to the local doctor and complains that he isn't worth a darn in bed anymore, just no luck at all, and his old but still eager wife has started to express some complaints. The doctor works out a program with some of the new fancy pills and potions and sends the old man home, saying, "There you go, Nels. You're going to be as good as a twenty-year-old in no time at all."

Nels goes home but is back at the doctor's office in a couple hours, saying, "I told my wife what you said, but she won't believe me."

"Well," the doctor says, "I can take care of that." He writes out a note on his official pad that reads, "Dear Mrs. Larsen—This is to certify that I have dosed Old Nels here, and I'm fixing him up good as new. In a couple weeks, if not days, he should be able to do about as well as he could when he was the young and strapping lad you met when you were a young girl."

Old Nels read the note over and said, "Doc, I wonder if you could do one more thing for me. Could you write out this note again, but instead of it saying 'Dear Mrs. Larsen,' could you just write 'To Whom It May Concern'?"

Sometimes the elderly simply have to make do with what makes do. An elderly gent goes in for an annual checkup and finds, as seems to be increasingly the case these days, that the doctor is not the grizzled old goat who was his standard country doctor but instead a gorgeous, young, recent graduate of medical school, who is gaining experience in a rural practice. At first he is reluctant to get out of his clothes and into the hospital gown, but after she explains that she is a highly trained professional and he has no reason to be the least bit embarrassed, he complies. She tells him, "Okay, now I'm going to check your prostate, so lie here on the table and relax." She then pulls up his gown, spreads his legs, and continues, "Now, I'm going to pull your organ up out of the way while I feel for your prostate. So take a deep breath and say 'ninety-nine,' which will give me time to complete the exam." The old man does what he can to relax as she proceeds as she described. And he says, "One . . . two . . . three . . ."

As mentioned, the effects of aging on male vitality have been an issue for a long time, so it isn't surprising that it has become a common motif in many jokes and jests . . . and that many efforts have been sought to find a cure.

An elderly bachelor farmer had been courting a neighbor widow for some years without managing to move ahead in the relationship. One day he went over to visit her, and she complained that she was having trouble with her bull. He didn't seem to be able to get anything done with the cows, so to speak. "Have you ever tried the brick treatment?" the man asked her.

"Why, no, I haven't," she said. "What the heck is the 'brick treatment'?"

The old man grabs a brick off the ground, crawls through the fence where the bull is lazing, grabs the bull around the neck, and proceeds to rub the bull's head just as hard as he can with the brick. "*That* is the brick treatment," he shouts to the widow who is looking on. "That should get him interested in the heifers again." Sure enough that bull sniffs the air, snorts, and starts to amble over to the heifers, showing an obvious interest again in what he had seemed to forget was his obligation.

The old widow watched it all. When the old man came back through the fence and headed back to the house, the widow said, "No wonder so many men around here are bald-headed."

Some geezers, meanwhile, are wilier than others. Bob, a seventy-year-old extremely wealthy widower, shows up at the town tavern with a breathtakingly beautiful twenty-five-year-old blonde who knocks everyone's socks off with her youthful sex appeal and charm. She hangs on Bob's arm and listens intently to his every word. His buddies at the tavern are all aghast. They manage to corner him alone and ask, "Bob, how'd you get the trophy girlfriend?"

Bob replies, "Girlfriend? She's my wife!"

They're knocked over and ask, "So how'd you persuade her to marry you?"

Bob says, "I lied about my age."

His friends respond, "So did you tell her you were only fifty?"

Bob smiles and says, "No, I told her I was ninety."

Ray Johnson, a local friend I introduced to you as the grocery storekeeper in an earlier story, told me a tale that is set in my own little village. When Ray retired from the business of selling vittles, he opened a small exercise and fitness center here called the Healthy Woman. (I have gotten myself into trouble now and then by referring to it as the Hefty Woman.) When the center was opened to men, one old-timer asked Ray, "Which machine will put me in good with someone like the hot young thing with the pony tail running on that treadmill over there?"

Ray responded, "That would be the ATM over at the tavern."

A standard story I hear regularly and in various forms tells of the old gent in town who was accused in a paternity suit brought by a lovely young woman in the town and pleaded guilty, but it was obvious to everyone and anyone who knew him that there was no way in billy hell that he could be the perpetrator. When his friends asked why on earth he had confessed and paid the penalty when he was innocent, he said, "The evidence was so darn flattering, I didn't have the heart to deny it."

On a different note, an elderly friend of mine with a young wife told me that his wife was pregnant although he had sworn that his days of raising children were long over, and I asked how he felt about the situation. Acknowledging he had made it so clear that he did not want any more children in his life, he said morosely, "Rog, I'd go out in the backyard and shoot myself if I weren't convinced I'd be murdering an innocent man."

I once talked to an ancient bachelor here in town and asked if he'd ever thought about getting married. He said, "Yep. I'm just looking for a rich old widow with a really bad cough." He was also, however, the one who told me he was then already so old that he didn't buy green bananas.

Ole and Old Sven vere talking about sex. Sven said, "Yassir, I did it tree times las night vit my tirty-year-old wife."

Ole replied, "You're kidding!! I can't even do it vonce anymore. Vat's your secret?"

"Vell," Sven replied, "da secret is to eat lotsa dat heavy home-style rye bread."

Ole yumped up and rushed as fast as he could to da store. He told the clerk, "I'd like four loaves of dat home-style rye bread like vat Sven buys."

The clerk said, "Dats a lotta rye bread; it'll probably get hard before you finish eating it all."

"Damn!" Ole said. "How does everyvone know about dis except me?!"

Men have searched through all of recorded history for a secret formula that would keep them ready for promising, uh, encounters with willing women. Today it's called "male enhancement for sexual activity," a term that once evoked the response from Linda—probably more revealing than I should confess, by the way—"What does it do? Make them shave and take a shower?"

When the question arose around the village about how a lovely young woman wound up with a grizzled old coot like me, the following story, reported to be an old favorite in earlier times, found new life in the Dannebrog Tavern.

Ol' Rog was walking along the main street one day when he spotted a buddy on the other side of the street, laughing and snuggling with a lovely young lady not seen before in town. When he had a chance, Rog cornered his friend and asked him how on earth he managed to land a prize like the woman he'd been seen with on Saturday. The friend helpfully explained, "Rog, if you want a woman like that, you'll have to do some major spiffing up. Get out of those overalls. Go down to Grand Island, and buy yourself some nice, new dress-up clothes. Shave every day and not just every other week or so like you usually do. Take a shower every morning, and sprinkle on a little foo-foo water. Keep that up for a while and just watch: you'll wind up with a woman like mine."

So Rog decided to give it a try. He scrapped the overalls and bought himself some fancy pants and a spiffy new sports coat. To everyone's astonishment he shaved every day, combed his hair, and sprinkled on imported foo-foo water, just as his friend had advised. And sure as heck, next thing you know, Rog was back in town with Lovely Linda on his arm, strutting down the main street as his buddy told him he would.

After a couple days, Rog was in town and strolling down the street in his new guise when all at once, out of nowhere, a bolt of lightning blasted out of the cloudless sky and struck Rog dead on the spot. Well, the first thing Rog did when he got to heaven was to march indignantly up to God and sputter, "Why ME? Why NOW?"

God shook his head sadly and said, "Sorry, Rog, didn't recognize you!"

Since I have already told you way more than I should have, my only recourse is to go even further and hope you imagine that I am only joking. Once a story on the evening television news discussed a new medication to enhance a woman's interest in sex. Linda watched the report and then said to no one in particular, "Yeah, right, like a woman is going to take *that*! What do they do—roll it into a chocolate ball and toss it into the air for her to catch in her mouth, hoping she'll swallow it whole?!" I pretended that I didn't hear her and was completely engrossed in reading my newspaper.

No end (as it were) of old-timers have told me that they do take Viagra . . . but only to keep themselves from rolling out of bed at night. And what about that curious caveat in every television advertisement for these medications that men who "experience an erection lasting over four hours should seek medical attention"? Just out of curiosity I once asked my physician and friend Bill Lawton if he'd ever had someone come to his office with that problem, and he laughed, "No, I sure haven't."

So I asked, "What would you do if a man came to your office with that kind of problem?"

Bill thought about it a minute and then said, probably reasonably, "I'd send him over to the nurses' station."

Here's a similar tale of misinterpreted intent: An old gent comes home one evening and presents his wife with a tube of KY jelly, saying, "Here's something to make you happy tonight." And it did. She put it on the bedroom doorknob, and since he couldn't get into the room, he spent the night sleeping on the sofa. I am also reminded of the pretended obscene riddling joke, What happened when the newlyweds mixed up the KY jelly with glazing putty? Their windows fell out.

And this following story, with genders reversed, includes

clearly modern elements that suggest civil ribaldry is still being generated today in American folk humor:

An elderly couple was lying in bed one evening as usual when the old man seemed to get a little frisky, fondling his wife as he hadn't in many years. He massaged her neck and then moved down her back, explored the length of her legs and arms, moved his hands under the top of her pajamas, and . . . well . . . more. But all at once to her surprise . . . and frustration . . . he stopped and rolled back over. "Honey, that was going so well. Why did you stop?" she asked.

"I found the remote," he said.

For reasons I am afraid to think too much about, I have always enjoyed stories about confusion in sexual matters. One that always rises to the surface is about the young man walking along the main street of town when he spots an old friend sitting on a bench, so he stops to chat a while. But as a young woman approaches, the old friend says, "Want to have some fun? Wait a minute and watch this." As the woman passes immediately before them the friend says, "Tickle your ass with a feather?"

The woman stops immediately, fixes an icy eye on him, and snarls, "What did you say?"

The fellow says, "Uh, I said, 'Typical Nebraska weather.'"

The woman thinks about it a moment, smiles, and says, "Yes, it certainly is," and walks on.

This scenario happens a couple of times when the newcomer to the game says, "That *does* look like fun. Let me give it a try."

So the two men sit on the bench and talk until another young woman comes walking along. Right on cue the young friend says, "Stick a feather up your butt?"

The woman stops and sputters with indignation, "What did you just say, young man?"

In confusion the fellow says, "Uuuuh . . . sure looks like rain!"

Callow Youth

The knowledge gap is not always just between a wife and her husband or a young woman and a geezer, but sometimes even it occurs between a young woman and a young man. It seems the male is outpaced intellectually, sexually, and carnally at every age.

I'm not even sure I understand what's funny about the earlier story involving feathers and weather, but for some reason I find the mildly unsettling story funny. I suspect we often laugh at stories we don't quite understand but that we *know* somehow are funny to others. One of the locals laughed at a joke in the café one day, and someone commented that it seemed strange that he was so amused because, being almost totally deaf, he probably didn't hear or understand much of the story let alone the punch line. When he was confronted with this curious behavior, he laughed again and admitted that he really hadn't heard the joke, but it just made him feel so good to see everyone else laughing that he just laughed along too.

If bewilderment about the mysteries of life, love, and sex are confusing for adults, we can only imagine how baffling they must be for children. The brilliant comedian Buddy Hackett was a storyteller of the old stripe even if he was raised in Brooklyn and can only be considered a modern performer in every sense. I once heard him tell a story that fits the mold of civil ribaldry nonetheless. He said that when he was a young boy, a terrible storm passed near his home, and afterward his father took the family out for an automobile ride to survey the damage. Somewhere along the way in the rural countryside Buddy happened to see a bull servicing a cow and innocently asked his father if the storm's winds had perhaps blown that bull up on top of the cow. His father, wanting to avoid explaining "the birds and the bees" at this point, stammered and stuttered and said, "Uh, no, Son, that's not what was going on there." Naturally enough, Buddy then asked what *was* going on. His father, flailing for something to say, muttered something about those animals "making brownies."

In his stage routine Buddy admitted that he gave that some considerable thought but figured his father must know best, so he didn't question the matter further. But a couple weeks later a young girl who was a school classmate of his called him on the phone and asked if he would like to come over to her house that afternoon to make some brownies. Buddy said he told her he would, but he didn't think the wind was blowing hard enough.

The frequency of such stories suggests that (1) children are inquisitive about sex, (2) they are confused about what they see and hear, and (3) parents—men in general and rural males in particular—are not the best references to turn to for accurate information about such matters. And sometimes it's hard to figure out when the dust settles who knows more and who knows less, the child or the father.

A guy from the city took his son to a farm and showed him what country life is like. On the farm the father took the lad to see some pigs. While they were standing there looking at them, two pigs started breeding, and as always seems to happen, the boy asked his father what was going on. The father didn't know what to say because he thought his son was too young to understand the facts of life, so he said, "Well, son, it's like this. The one pig broke his foot, and the other pig is being nice and helping him walk."

The boy thought about it for a while and then got a strange look on his face. He said, "That's terrible."

The father didn't understand because he thought he had given a great explanation. So he asked the boy, "What's so terrible about it?"

The lad replied, "Isn't that just like life? You try to be nice to a guy, and that's what he does to you."

The moment when a father or mother is called upon to have the birds-and-bees conversation with a child is an experience many parents share. So it is not surprising that a rich inventory of stories have arisen about the circumstances and their results. In my case it came as unexpectedly as it always seems to do. My son Chris came to me one day and asked me to explain what prostitution is. I did my best to explain the activity as circumspectly and yet as honestly as I could, probably sweating bullets and stammering through what was likely an incoherent lecture. When I finished, Chris looked at me, still puzzled, and asked, "But . . . then why is Perry Mason always arguing with the prostitution?" At that point I remembered I had some pressing issue or another I had to deal with elsewhere.

The normal expectation is that a child remains innocent of the facts of life and offensive language and maintains a certain level of respect (if not fear!) of his or her elders and authority. One therefore expects humor about childhood innocence. A common motif in folk humor centers on an ordinary childhood behavior—that is, the natural inclination at some point to "play doctor" with a willing participant of the opposite sex. Usually an associated story will have the astonished male gasping upon being granted the wished peek, "Oh, my god! They cut your wienie off!" Or perhaps, "So *that*'s the difference between Catholics and Baptists!"

The following is an example of the child wise beyond her years and a refreshing relief from the far more common Little Johnny stories.

Little Sally came home from school with a smile on her face and told her mother, "Mom, guess what! Frankie Brown showed me his weenie today behind the school." Before the mother could express concern, Sally went on to say, "It reminded me of a peanut."

Relaxing a bit, Sally's mother said, "Because it's so small?"

Sally replied, "No, because it's salty."

A common story in Dannebrog tells about the time a city family visited a cousin's farm and happened upon a stallion that seemed to be having prurient thoughts about some mare in his past or perhaps in his future. The boy pointed at the monstrous member hanging beneath the stallion and asked with wide eyes, "What's *that*?"

"Oh, nothing," muttered the embarrassed mother.

Whereupon the father added, "But then your mother's spoiled."

Age Has Nothing to Do with It

Within the genre of the ribald tale there exists a balance. The story's humor depends on surprise—perhaps a woman who knows far too much about men and/or sex, or far too little; or a child who knows too much or too little; or one member of a couple who wants too much bedtime activity or too little. So just as I have given examples of women who surprise their partners with an unsettling sophistication about sex, there are those who know laughingly little or are remarkably ill informed. Following are some examples of each variety, starting with women young and old who know more than expected.

A fellow who thinks he is pretty smart takes the neighbor girl out in the barn to fool around in the haymow and pushes hard to accomplish the big one, if you know what I mean. But the young lady protests that she won't cooperate unless he promises to marry her. "Look here," he argues, "if I were buying a cow, I would want a sample of her milk before I closed the deal. If I were buying a horse, I'd want to give her a test ride before shaking hands on the deal. If I were buying a dog, I'd want to see how he hunts before laying out the cash. Now, if we're talking marriage, I want a sample of the merchandise before we close the bargain."

"No," the girl insists, slipping back into her clothes. "There won't be any samples. But I can get you plenty of references."

I was once regaling a group of my cronies with stories

about some of my adventures in my younger years, and one of my friends said, "Welsch, is there *anything* you won't do?" And Linda remarked, considerably enhancing her reputation in my circle of friends, "I'll tell you a few things he won't do." So civil ribaldry dealing with the woman who has surprising knowledge is not at all far fetched even in true life. One can't help but wonder how many of these stories told as jokes and folktales might indeed have originated as actual events and started as anecdotes or even oral history (as it were) before becoming traditional lore.

A new bride complains to her mother that her young groom seems insatiable in the bedroom. He won't let her out of bed in the morning, comes home for lunch and a romp in bed at noon, and is rarin' for more when he comes home from the fields in the evening. Her mother says, "Sounds to me like you could use some saltpeter."

"Oh gosh," sputtered the girl, "once you try the fresh stuff, Mom, you'll never go back to the salted kind!"

So much for women not having a sense of humor. A close friend of mine told me that before he got married he went to his venerable grandmother both to tell her about his plans and to ask her permission and counsel. He returned from the conversation with glazed eyes and shaken confidence. He said she told him, "Never take up with a woman with big hands, Dave. Never." Before he could gather his wits and ask why, she explained, "They'll make your pecker look small." And she laughed uproariously.

Conversely, there is no shortage of tales about women who live in ignorance when it comes to the ways of sex, at least when it comes to their own children.

Three mothers are talking about their daughters. The first one says, "I was looking through my daughter's things the other day and found cigarettes. I can't believe my daughter smokes!"

The second woman says, "Ladies, I was looking through

my daughter's things, and I found a bottle of whiskey. I can't believe my daughter drinks."

The third says, "I was going through my daughter's things, and I found a pack of condoms. I can't believe my daughter has a penis!"

Even though males are most often depicted as the outwitted or clueless boobs in these folktales (remembering, though, that it has been my experience . . . probably distorted by my own gender . . . that they are told primarily by males), sometimes even men and boys shine through with wit, knowledge, conquest, and justice.

An elderly gentleman got on the train and sat down in the last available seat, one between two women. At the next depot a young woman got on the train and stood in the aisle a while, looking for a seat. Being considerate, the old gent said to the young woman, "You can sit on my lap, dear. I'm an old man. You have nothing to be afraid of." The woman said thanks but no. A few minutes later the man repeated his offer, but the woman again politely declined the offer. After a short time the man made his offer a third time, and since she was getting tired of standing and being jostled as the trained rumbled along, this time she accepted and settled down on the old man's lap. A few minutes later, however, the old fellow said, "Lady, excuse me, but you'd better get back up. I guess I'm not as old as I thought I was."

Most stories about old age lament its afflictions and the decline in energies and vitality it brings with it. But now and then we are offered hope.

An old fart was once asked how it came to be that he lived to be more than a hundred years old. "I ate like a pig," he started. "And I drank a quart of good whiskey . . . or bad whiskey . . . every day. I smoked a cigar whenever I felt like it, morning and evening, and I never missed a chance to corner the hired girl out in the barn. And that's why I've lived so long."

Shocked, the interviewer said, "Just a minute. I had an uncle who did things like that, and he died when he was fifty-two. Raising that kind of hell sure didn't give him a long life."

"Well," reasoned the old-timer, "I guess he just didn't do it long enough."

As a common phrase in geezerly circles has it these days, "A shot in the glass is better than a shot in the ass." To wit: A bunch of reporters had gathered in a ninety-seven-year-old man's hospital room to interview him on the occasion of his birthday. The nurses pulled aside the oxygen tent for a little while, and the interviewers asked him to what he attributed such a good, long life. "I never fooled around with women, for one thing," he gasped. "I never smoked cigars, and I never let alcohol cross my lips."

About that time there was a terrible crash from the hospital room next door, then screaming, yelling, and loud laughter. One of the reporters asked, "What the heck is *that* all about?"

The old man grunted, "Oh, I suppose that's my drunken, hell-raisin' father chasin' the nurses around the bed again!"

Innocent? Or Simply Not Guilty?

There are clear categories of double entendre–based dialogue jokes reflecting the kind of humorous combat found in the exchange between the traveler from the city (or perhaps the North) with the rural (perhaps southern) fiddler in the Arkansas Traveler but with at least one of the protagonists being a child. While all of these humorous dialogues are based on wordplay that often includes a reluctant prurience on the part of one of the persons in the exchange—usually the one who is expected or presumes to be the more properly behaved—they often demonstrate a conflict between the generations and the sexes. In my experience the common formats are the Little Johnny stories, which feature a precocious schoolboy who, when pressed with classroom questions, turns the tables on his teacher and sometimes the principal of the school with his answers to the teacher's questions or perhaps with a series of questions of his own. They all seem innocent enough but suggest a knowledge well beyond the expectations of the adults in the scenario.

Many of the individual question-and-answer combinations in the following dialogues appear individually as a genre called pretended obscene riddle. They are interesting because the burden of prurience is thrust upon not only the teacher, or "Miss Brooks," and the principal in these constructions but also the person who is hearing the joke.

Perhaps the real question for the folklorist is, are these indeed *pretended* obscenities when it is clear that the questions and answers would never occur in normal conversation were it not for the intention of provoking titillation, embarrassment, or prurient satisfaction? The dialogues as I present them here are interesting too because they overlap with civil ribaldry; there's not a curse word in the lot. Also, while they are always transmitted orally as individual ripostes—that is, as "folklore"—when they are assembled into dialogues, they are more often transmitted in print perhaps now as Xeroxlore or weblore and sometimes become folklore when sent from one person to another and to another or become more a part of popular culture when presented as e-zine items or website offerings. In the Little Johnny exchanges we recognize one element of folklore—distribution over some extended space and/or time—in the name of the teacher. Or am I perhaps the only one who still recalls Eve Arden's radio, movie, and television character from *Our Miss Brooks*?

A first-grade teacher, Miss Brooks was having trouble with her student Little Johnny. So she asked him, "Johnny, what is your problem?"

Little Johnny said, "Teacher, I'm too smart for the first grade. My sister is in the third grade, and I'm smarter than she is! I think I should be in the third grade too! At least. Maybe even sixth!"

Miss Brooks had had enough. So she took Johnny to the principal's office. While Little Johnny waited in the outer office, Miss Brooks explained to the principal what the situation was. The principal told Miss Brooks he would give the boy a test, and if he failed to answer any of his questions, he was to go back to the first grade and behave. She agreed. Little Johnny was brought in, and after they explained the conditions to him, he agreed to take the test.

THE PRINCIPAL [*looking Little Johnny solemnly in the eye*]: What is three times three?

LITTLE JOHNNY [*confidently*]: Nine.

THE PRINCIPAL: What is six times six?

LITTLE JOHNNY: Thirty-six.

And so it went with every question the principal thought a third grader should know.

THE PRINCIPAL: I think Little Johnny is right. He should be in the third grade.

MISS BROOKS: Let me ask him some questions.

THE PRINCIPAL AND LITTLE JOHNNY: Agreed.

MISS BROOKS: What does a cow have four of that I have only two of?

LITTLE JOHNNY: Legs.

MISS BROOKS: What do you have in your pants that I don't have in mine?

LITTLE LOHNNY [*eyeing the principal's shock*]: Pockets.

MISS BROOKS: What does a dog do that a man steps in?

LITTLE JOHNNY: Pants.

MISS BROOKS: What starts with a C and ends with a T, is hairy, oval, and delicious?

LITTLE JOHNNY: Coconut.

MISS BROOKS: What goes in hard and pink comes out soft and sticky?

LITTLE JOHNNY: Bubblegum.

MISS BROOKS: What does a man do standing up, a woman do sitting down, and a dog do on three legs?

LITTLE JOHNNY: Shake hands.

MISS BROOKS [*exasperated*]: Okay, Little Johnny, now I will ask some "Who am I?" sort of questions.

LITTLE JOHNNY: Yep. Fire away!

MISS BROOKS: You stick your pole in me. You tie me down to get me up. I get wet before you do. Who am I?

LITTLE JOHNNY: You're a tent.

MISS BROOKS: Your finger goes in me. You play with me when you're bored. The best man always had me first.

LITTLE JOHNNY: You're a wedding ring.

MISS BROOKS: I have a stiff shaft. My tip penetrates. I come with a quiver.

LITTLE JOHNNY: You're an arrow.

MISS BROOKS: What word starts with an F, ends with a K, and means a lot of heat and excitement?

LITTLE JOHNNY: Fire truck.

THE PRINCIPAL [*breathing a huge sigh of relief*]: Miss Brooks, go ahead and put him in the sixth grade. I got almost all the answers wrong myself.

A factor rarely considered in examining such folklore materials is the role of the audience, or the persons (or person, since as often as not such "jokes" are told from one person to another) who are told the story. Presumably, like the school principal, that listener will consider the worst understanding of the boy's questions and responses and thus be confronted with the reality of his or her own prurient thoughts.

Folk humor, traditional narrative, and the joke exist, as I have noted, in a large corpus of materials in which there are few natural or distinct boundaries, with one genre fading indistinguishably into others. It would therefore perhaps be useful to note some of the joke forms surrounding that of civil ribaldry that are related to or may seem related to or which may even be confused with the genre. Civil ribaldry functions to deal with ribald materials in an inoffensive way, but other traditional humor forms approach the problem in another way.

Here's a similar teacher–Little Johnny dialogue that I have seen conveyed with the "Miss Brooks" characterization.

A teacher was helping her students with math. She recited the following word problem: "There are three birds sitting on a wire. A hunter shoots one of the birds. How many birds are left on the wire?"

Little Johnny holds up his hand and says, "None."

"No, no, no. That's incorrect, Little Johnny. Let's try again," the teacher says patiently. She holds up three fingers. "There are *three* birds sitting on a wire. A hunter shoots one," she says as she puts down one finger, "so how many birds are left on the wire?"

"None," the boy says again with authority.

The teacher sighs. "Little Johnny, please tell me how you came up with that answer."

"It's simple," says the boy. "When the hunter shoots one bird, the others fly away."

"Well," she says, "okay. That's not technically correct, but I like the way you think."

"Okay," chimes Little Johnny. "Now let me ask you a question. There are three women sitting on a bench eating popsicles. One woman is licking her popsicle, one woman is biting hers, and the third one is sucking the popsicle. Which one is married?"

Miss Brooks looks at the boy's angelic face and turns three shades of red.

"C'mon, Miss Brooks," Little Johnny urges impatiently. "One woman is licking the popsicle, one is biting, and one is sucking. Which one is married?"

"Well," she gulps, writhes in discomfort, and in a barely audible whisper replies uncertainly, "the one who's sucking?"

"No," he says. "The one wearing the wedding ring. But I like the way you think."

Within tradition, humorous dialogues set in an interrogatory context approach being an altogether separate genre.

In these pages I have already presented the Arkansas Traveler vignette and the "trial" in the principal's office. Scattered throughout I have used stories to illustrate other points that use a courtroom as a setting. A widespread motif incorporates marital conflict as a courtroom scene. The following example also uses the standard folk persona of Ole and Lena, and it is therefore recited with what the storyteller presumes to be a Minnesota or Wisconsin Scandinavian accent, often funny enough in itself. In some versions the warring couple is speaking to an attorney; sometimes they are appearing before a judge. The negotiator asks questions to determine the nature of the conflict and resolve the issues.

LAWYER/JUDGE: Do you have grounds for a divorce?

OLE AND/OR LENA: Oh yes, we have fifty acres.

LAWYER/JUDGE: Lena, does he beat you?

LENA: Every time.

LAWYER/JUDGE: Ole, do you have a grudge?

OLE: No, but we got a nice pole shed.

LAWYER/JUDGE: What are your relations like?

LENA: I like his in-laws better than mine.

LAWYER/JUDGE: Has there been infidelity in your marriage?

OLE: Both my son and daughter have stereos, but to be honest I don't like der kind of music at all.

LAWYER/JUDGE: Please, I'm trying to determine here if you have a case!

OLE AND/OR LENA: We got no Case. We like dem orange Allis-Chalmers!

LAWYER/JUDGE: Enough of this. Why do you want this divorce?

OLE AND LENA IN UNISON: Because it's impossible to have an intelligent conversation wit dat old fool!

JUDGE: I've heard enough. The divorce is granted, and, Ole, I'm going to give Lena four hundred dollars a month for support.

OLE: Vell, dat's mighty generous of you, Your Honor. And every once in a while I'll chip in a few bucks myself!

The examples of Miss Brooks, the precocious lad Little Johnny, and Ole and Lena in divorce court certainly demonstrate the central character of civil ribaldry in that they are clearly suggestive, if not outright obscene. Not typical of the genre, however, are other factors—extended dialogue (and yet they are "tales," which is to say narratives) and a lack of clear rural elements, without seeming restricted to a Plains inventory even in a general way. Nonetheless, they are a cognate form and show the strong motif typical of civil ribaldry in presenting the indelicate delicately. Sort of.

It is interesting when such combative dialogue is presented as a mini drama, complete with its own stage setting, but oral combat is a strong element in many cultural contexts, from high opera to television situation comedies, from blues songs to rock and roll. No less in contemporary folklore, especially as with the examples featuring Ole and Lena, it figures highly in the eternal battle of the sexes.

Combative language has been studied extensively, especially in American black culture where "The Dozens" became an art during the last half of the twentieth century while remaining a mystery to most non-African Americans. The Dozens' verbal jousting often centered on sexual, incestual references about the opponents' female relatives, especially the mother, and reflected a wider culture of gender wars that still persist in American culture's "blonde jokes." The blondes in question are always female, of course.

A blonde takes her malfunctioning automobile to a mechanic, who fixes it, and tells her the car had only a minor problem and that it's now running fine. When she asks what the problem was, he answers, "Crap in the carburetor."

And she asks in turn, "And how often do I need to do that?"

It stands to reason, I suppose, that the gender-specific jokes I hear are always directed toward women. I suspect, however, that there is an entirely separate and rich tradition among women that aims the broadsides in the opposite direction. I am fortunate to have some female friends who have been willing to share their own verbal lore with me. I am absolutely certain there is more, and worse. Or better, as the case may be.

MAN: God, why did you make woman so beautiful?

GOD: So you would love her.

MAN: But why did you make her so stupid?

GOD: So she would love you.

Other Unmentionables

The bulk of the materials I have presented in these pages, as suggested by the word "ribald," is sensitive because of the sexual content. But other topics too are held to be sensitive in our culture and therefore invite "civil" presentations, especially when they are dealt with in humorous stories. In earlier chapters I've mentioned some of those nonsexual but sensitive topics—defecation and religion, for example. In our culture, and in many others, the idea of death is also handled with circumspection. We don't even like to say the word "death," so we tap-dance around it with such terms as "passed away," "expired," "departed," "gave up the ghost," "is no longer with us," or, less respectfully, "kicked the bucket." We might therefore think that death is scarcely a suitable topic for humor, yet here in the following examples it is complete too with the continuing motif of the battle of the sexes. One tale is so commonplace in my village that one can evoke the entire story and its content with a simple phrase: "Easy, boys, easy."

The shrewish wife of a local man dies, and everyone in the community presumes the obvious—that is, while folks may show at least a demonstration of grief, they certainly also feel a good deal of relief for the old gent. At the close of the funeral, the pallbearers carry the coffin down the front stairs of the church when, to the horror of everyone looking on, the front two carriers stumble. In the flurry of flailing arms and legs, the coffin tumbles to the ground and falls open. Even more dramatically, the "deceased" sits up in the coffin, jarred back to life by the fall and concussion! Revived, the shrewish wife and her beleaguered husband return to the farm to, uh, enjoy another five years of marital blitz [*sic*].

When the woman dies later—this time for real—the husband arranges another funeral. Again the pallbearers bring the harridan's coffin down the church's front steps, where the widower is heard to mutter softly but firmly, "Easy, boys, easy."

Similarly, and perhaps on the same occasion, the graveside service had just barely finished when there was a blinding flash of lightning, followed by a tremendous clap of thunder. The old widower looked at the preacher and calmly said, "Well, she's there."

A genial friend of mine lost his first and wonderful wife after a long, long life, and Linda and I were discussing gingerly the similarities of this situation with another that we had seen occur just a few years earlier. In the earlier case another genial, generous, beloved friend had loved an occasional beer with the boys, was a sought-after card player, and could always be counted on for a good story. He had remarried and found himself a virtual captive in his own home, removed from everything he loved and forced instead into company and contexts that clearly made him one miserable fellow.

As I watched the same thing happen with another friend, I said to Linda, "I sure hope Bernie isn't getting himself into the same miserable situation that George wound up suffering, living the rest of his life in misery."

And Linda said, "I don't see why Bernie should be any different from the rest of you." Gulp.

The relief felt at some funerals may be mutual. In the midst of yet another long and loud domestic disturbance, the Old Man yells at his constant antagonist, "When you die, the tombstone I put on your grave is going to say, 'Here lies my old wife—cold as ever'!"

Thereupon his wife, at least his equal in the confrontation, retorts, "And when you finally give me relief and die, I'm putting a stone over you that says, 'Here lies my husband—stiff at last'!"

On the contrary, some stories about marital respect extend well beyond the natural end of a long marriage. A story in Dannebrog tells about an old farmer's wife dying and the community being amazed when the old man almost immediately marries Sarah, the pretty hired girl who is half his age. During the wedding night a bunch of the local rowdies get together and decide to have a *chivaree* for the newlyweds. They head over to the old man's farm, where they set up the customary hullabaloo, shooting off guns, banging on bucket bottoms, hooting and hollering, and knocking against the barn walls. They hoped to rouse the old man and get him to come out, where they would offer to give him a night of peace in exchange for a generous round of good whiskey.

After a while the old gent comes storming out of the house, still pulling on his overalls, and yells, "What the hell is wrong with you crazy people, raising a ruckus like this so soon after the funeral?!"

As is so often the case, what's sauce for the goose is indeed also sauce for the gander and is illustrated in the following story, which is often told in central Nebraska. It features chocolate chip cookies, but it is also variously told with the treat being kolaches, fry bread, runzas, or *kringeles*, depending on the ethnicity of the narrator.

An elderly man is on his deathbed when wafting from the kitchen into his room he smells the aroma of his favorite chocolate chip cookies. With his remaining strength, he pulls himself together, rises up from the bed, gets to his feet, and slowly, painfully shuffles his way out of the bedroom and into the kitchen. And sure enough, on the kitchen table is a pile of his beloved cookies. For a moment he wonders if his beloved wife has gone to this effort to rouse his spirits, restore his vitality, and nourish his inner man or perhaps to give him some comfort in his last moments. Or perhaps . . . has he already died and gone to heaven?

With another moment of great exertion he staggers to the table and with a shaking hand reaches to grasp the nearest cookie, when suddenly a spatula smacks him across the hand and a stern voice scolds, "Don't even think of it, old man. Those are for the funeral."

An Afterword

Okay, how many times as you read these stories did you say, "That's an old story, one I've heard it a thousand times"? Or "I wonder why Rog left out the story about [fill in the blank]?" Well, I'll tell you why. First, these stories are folklore—that is, informally transmitted tales that have been around a while and have covered some distance, thereby gaining some polish. They have been told numerous times because they are good stories; in a kind of circular logic, the reason they are good stories is because they have been told a lot. And really, are they any less funny for having been told so often before?

In my dotage I've thought about having cards printed saying "Stop me if I've told you this one before" because I know (Linda has commented!) that I tend to tell the same stories over and over. She is a painter, so she sees the world in terms of visual vignettes; I'm a storyteller and live in a context of one story after another. Which I like to tell. And retell. Just as her studio is stacked with studies and variations of a single theme painted dozens of times, I tell the same story again and again because I like the story and perhaps because I've noted that people like to hear it.

We like to hear the same story repeatedly if it is told well. From childhood we have our favorite stories and insist that our parents and grandparents tell us those same stories over and over, necessarily without variation. It isn't enough that it be generally the same story; it has to be retold word for word. There is an old canard that there are only seven stories, which are retold throughout all of human history. Willa Cather narrows her count even further: "There are only two or three human stories, and they go on repeating themselves as fiercely as if they had never happened before; like the larks in this country, that have been singing the same five notes over for thousands of years" (*O Pioneers!*, part 2, chapter 4). In my own *The Reluctant Pilgrim*, I note my surprise in finding that the story of the wandering pilgrim who seeks the truth in a predictable inventory of experiences—wealth and commerce, religious immersion, sex and indulgence, learning, nature, and so on—and, in the end, returns to find it where he first started, his home, is a widespread motif complex throughout literary history.

No one protests when an example of civil ribaldry, many of which I have presented here, is reintroduced in a conversation, especially if someone in the circle has not heard the tale before. Often as not that person has been me, and I have seen the delight in others as the surprise conclusion of the narrative dawns on me and I explode in laughter. Hopefully that has been your experience in these pages. Sure, some of them are old-timers, and you may well have heard them before, perhaps in another variation, but, well, I present them here again. And this time I tell them as I have heard them and pass them along to you.

The reason your favorite story or the story your father told or the story you heard at the café this morning is *not* here is because, as I haven't heard every story that's been told, there's a good chance I haven't heard it yet. Or since I am seventy-eight years old at this writing, I did hear your story and loved it, but somewhere along the line it got lost in my brain or the bar napkin I wrote it on went through our washing machine and I couldn't reconstruct it. I'd love to hear it again. Feel free to send it along to Post Office

Box 187, Dannebrog, Nebraska 68831, and maybe it will show up in this book's sequel, *Son of Why I'm an Only Child.*

I have moreover omitted some stories because I simply cannot include them all; therefore, I have cited those tales that I think are good examples of what I want to illustrate. Nor is there a doubt in my mind that within days of the publication of this book, I will hear one . . . maybe two . . . even three new and wonderful examples of civil ribaldry that absolutely belong in these pages but aren't here. We work with what we have.

As with the study of tall tales, however, it is not the precision with which the text was recorded but the essence of its poetic content that lets one admire it as a work of art. In some peripheral way I suppose a precisely transcribed example of folklore offers material for scientific analysis that a more casual rendition such as those I include here may not. But the constrictions of field collection make such precise collection next to impossible. In fact, whatever scientific rigor may profit from precise transcriptions may be lost in the clumsiness of the fieldworker's fumbling with a tape recorder or notepad. No, here I was simply a member of the crowd, lucky enough to be present when stories were told. My appreciation was as much in my laughter as in any insight to the processes of folklore or the peculiarities of the respective era or geography.

I hope that in these pages you have seen a few of the reasons why my life changed when I was presented with the idea of folklore. I was in graduate school, studying languages. I loved languages and still do, but I was less enthusiastic about what went with linguistic studies: literature, fine arts, elegant culture, and other highfalutin stuff. But then I took a course in German Romanticism. The professor was without question the worst teacher I encountered in all my years of higher education, but something he talked about started a small fire in my soul. You see, the Romantics didn't find their inspiration in individual genius or elevated taste; they were interested in the kinds of songs and stories they found in rural and peasant cultures, the kinds of tales passed along by word of mouth. You know, folklore!

That notion hit me like a ton of bricks, because it occurred to me (I was not a fast learner!) that in the German community of Lincoln, Nebraska, I had grown up with the very elements that had inspired the Grimm brothers, Heinrich Heine, Johann Baptist Rousseau, and the others I was studying in my university classes. That is, wow! My "Rooshen" people had culture! Not the stuff of art galleries, concert halls, and university classes, but culture nonetheless. So I restarted my education and studied folklore. And I began writing about what I found.

Not only did folklore speak to my own heritage but also it permitted me to follow another inclination of mine, a resistance to specialization and an urge to follow the next wacky interest that came along the way. Just as the high and fine arts have many dimensions—law, medicine, literature, music, philosophy, art—the very same dimensions can be found in folklore. This breadth of subjects has allowed me to study, collect, write, and enjoy everything from folk art (in quilts, for example, or Scandinavian wood carving) to folk music and song, folk architecture, folk belief and custom, folk foodways, and . . . folktales such as the ones you have read in this collection. This remarkable latitude of interests is why some scholars prefer the term "folklife" rather than simply folk*lore*, because "lore" denotes to some only verbal materials while modern folklore studies include material culture, or the making of objects and perhaps transmitting information not with words but by example.

The stories I have labeled "civil ribaldry" are one small part—I suppose one could argue not even a particularly important part—of the larger body of traditional materials; nonetheless, they are a part that has interested me. I hope they not only amuse you but also remind you how important these informally transmitted materials are to our greater American, perhaps Great Plains, culture. I have also felt it is important to record and preserve this genre of folktale because as with the sophisticated arts and culture, folk culture too is constantly undergoing a transformation. There are not many people left who, as my parents did, find proverbs a useful way to express what they consider to be the collective wisdom. Authentic "folk" music (in quotes because it is not folklore at all now but almost always the product of individual creativity and transmitted only by radio, television, recording, and formal performance) is very rare in current American society, except perhaps in small ethnic enclaves. The joke, though, persists. Hang round the watercooler or spa locker room, and chances are you'll hear the latest joke almost every day. For the moment, at least, the joke is a dominant form of American folklore.

But even within that category are styles, fads, and tastes that are in constant flux. One day it's Ole and Lena jokes, then jokes about dumb blondes, how many whatevers it takes to screw in a light bulb, political jibes, and now those fumbles that some throwback, as I am, has with modern social media. That this dimension of our culture is alive and dynamic is exciting to me too; our folklore is constantly changing because it is as alive as it has ever been. On the one hand, some forms fade and disappear; no one has barn raisings any more except maybe some Amish communities, but even then they are a curiosity. I studied and wrote a book about the sod house; no one builds sod houses in the twenty-first-century. On the other hand, I also studied straw baled construction, a process that appeared on the Plains in the nineteenth century and then disappeared as the need for such construction techniques faded. Then—wow!—upon publication of my articles about *historical* straw bale construction in *The Whole Earth Catalog* and of my book

Shelter (1973), a new interest in the folk architectural form arose, not because folks lacked other materials this time but for ecological reasons.

As Pete Seeger wrote in his 1950s song (NOT a folksong!) "Turn, Turn, Turn," which was then popularized by the Limeliters and the Byrds, there truly is a season. The lyrics are almost a literal lift from chapter 3 of the book of Ecclesiastes, and Seeger turned them two millennia later into a pseudo folksong that then became a pop-culture recording hit. All cultural forms rise and fall, change, disappear, reappear . . . I offer this collection of Plains civil ribaldry in that spirit. Although there are deep historical roots for the "slightly naughty tale," from Geoffrey Chaucer and William Shakespeare and Giovanni Boccaccio to communities in which it has flourished and can still be found, it too may fade before whatever new folk humor form arises.

Well, so it goes. I have enjoyed the stories that my family and members of my adopted community of Dannebrog, Nebraska, have told. I have done my share of oral transmission because I enjoy not only hearing them but also telling them. In this collection I may be dealing with an endangered species, but it is not yet the stuff of paleontology. I'm betting I hear more stories in this coming year, perhaps quite a few more once this collection appears in print. But for the moment I am content to offer a window into the genre for people who either have not encountered it before or perhaps, as I did, knew of it but previously hadn't considered it as a distinct and interesting cultural form.

I'll be listening for the stories. You'll find me at the Big Table in the Dannebrog Tavern or maybe at Tom's on pizza night or at the Co-op with the usual morning loafers. I'll be trying desperately to remember the story I just heard or scribbling it down on a paper napkin, which I will then try to decipher after it goes through the washing machine and winds up in the dryer's lint trap.

CPSIA information can be obtained
at www.ICGtesting.com
Printed in the USA
LVOW11s0150101017
551771LV00003B/346/P